To Billie,

Thank you
a fan! Truly hope you
enjoy the book! :)

The Instrument of Darkness

Rusty Harding

The Instrument of Darkness is a work of fiction. Names, characters and incidents are products of the author's imagination or are used fictitiously. Any resemblance to actual events or locales or persons, living or dead, is entirely coincidental.

Published 2003 by
The Fiction Works
Lake Tahoe, Nevada
www.fictionworks.com

Copyright © 2002
by Rusty Harding

All rights reserved. No part of this book may be reproduced or transmitted in any form or by any electronic or mechanical means, including photo-copying, recording or by any information storage and retrieval system, without the written permission of the Publisher, except where permitted by law.

ISBN 1-58124-708-7
Printed in the
United States of America

History records that John Wilkes Booth, the slayer of Abraham Lincoln, was shot to death in a burning tobacco shed in April of 1865. But what if history were wrong? What if Booth survived that blazing barn, part of an assassination plot hatched by Lincoln's own cabinet?

Granbury, Texas, 1876: A flamboyant bartender named John St. Helen lies deathly ill. He summons his best friend to his bedside and begins to weave an incredible tale of murder, mystery, and historical deceit. And before his story is finished, John St. Helen will reveal the truth: that he is John Wilkes Booth, the Instrument of Darkness.

"This story is a work of fiction. While it does portray actual personages, it is not intended to be a historical treatise, nor is it the authoritative version of the assassination of Abraham Lincoln. The story is based on published theories, historical speculation, and American legend; most notably that of John St. Helen, a Texas bartender who made the astonishing yet compelling claim that he was actually the infamous John Wilkes Booth."

— Rusty Harding

"To my wife, Debra — for her love and infinite patience — this book is lovingly dedicated . . ."

Chapter One

All the world's a stage
And all the men and women merely players;
They have their exits and their entrances,
And one man in his time plays many parts . . .
~~~As You Like It~~~

Granbury, Texas - September, 1876

The note was lodged between the wall and a bottom corner of my message box, just beneath the lacquered shingle that proclaimed, Finis Bates, Attorney, and in my fatigue I nearly missed it.

"Come quick." it read tersely. *"Mr. St. Helen is desperately ill, and he asks to see you."*

The note was signed by Mrs. Grady, the woman who ran the boardinghouse over on Pearl Street where John St. Helen kept his lodgings. I reasoned she must have sent it over by her youngest son, Billy, owing partly to the odd locale—the highest an eight-year-old's arms could reach, no doubt—but mostly because I knew the dear widow rarely ventured out on her own, especially if she had boarders in residence. For someone whose very livelihood depended on a hostelry, she was an incredibly mistrusting soul.

I had just returned to Granbury after an arduous day in Glen Rose, where I had spent the entire day in court. A client of mine, a cattleman from southern Somervell County, had gotten himself into a rather nasty dispute with his neighbor over grazing boundaries. Being a man of significant wealth but disproportionate common sense—a not uncommon condition among many of his ilk, I am grieved to say—he had elected to arbitrate the matter with a Colt's revolver. A fellow rancher had nearly died, however, and it took all of my legal finagling to convince the judge that the entire affair was merely an exaggerated misunderstanding. Although he faced a two-year prison term, my client escaped with only a five-hundred-dollar fine, a sentence for which most rational men would have gleefully sung their lawyer's praises. But my reward was an immediate dismissal, along with a vehement warning to avoid future sojourns into Somervell County, especially if I wished to remain in decent health. Texas gratitude truly knew no bounds.

I crumpled the note and wearily tossed it aside, then started to go on in to a waiting and welcome bed. But something suddenly made me stop. St. Helen was my friend, and despite my exhaustion, I felt I should pay him at least a brief call. I did not believe for a moment that he was deathly ill, regardless of the note's urgency, for there was hardly a man in Granbury as robust and vigorous as John St. Helen. But it had been several weeks since I had last seen him, and his company might at least help to shake off the frustrated melancholy that had settled over me like the journey's dust.

I turned and trotted back down the steps that led to the rooms, both office and lodgings, that I kept above the Masonic Lodge there on Crockett Street. Granbury was nearly deserted, that close to sundown, and I shared the courthouse square with only a mongrel dog, a statue of General John Bell Hood, and a jovially whistling Negro workman. The black was busy hauling down the Lone Star flag, and I had to shake my head in genuine bemusement. Here it was nearly two years after Reconstruction had finally ended, and the Stars and Stripes had yet to make an official appearance above Hood County's brand-new stone edifice. The county, named for the aforementioned Texas Brigade warrior himself, teemed with Confederate veterans like a hound with fleas, and there were still many who refused to believe the Confederacy had truly died. I myself did not share their convictions, although, while merely a transplant to Texas from my native Tennessee, I fully understood the bitterness the war had left behind. Just like the terrible wounds inflicted by gun and saber, certain scars would never heal.

The Black Hawk Saloon, where John St. Helen worked as a bartender, stood at the corner of Crockett and Pearl, and I cast it a speculative glance as I passed by, recalling the first time the two of us had met nearly four years before. St. Helen had been a barkeep then, in fact, in his own tavern down in Glen Rose, and it was his profession which actually brought us together. St. Helen had bought a small saloon and dry goods store from a former Confederate soldier, who had neglected to tell the new owner that the whiskey and beer he profitably poured had been served without a state license. When the Austin authorities, Unionists all, finally caught the error, it was St. Helen who faced the threatened penalties. He came to me as an honest businessman, sincerely wanting to set the matter right. There was only one stipulation. St. Helen was unwilling, and almost vehemently so, to appear personally in a Yankee court of law.

I suppose I knew from that moment that there was something seriously wrong, some mysterious aspect of John St. Helen's past that he wanted desperately kept secret. Yet in all honesty, I cared very little. In my profession, especially during those terrible days of Reconstruction, I had yet to meet the man who hadn't had a skeleton or two hidden from the Unionists. The war had turned even the most saintly of souls into scalawags and misfits, at least from a Yankee perspective, and I knew better than to try and open such painful wounds. Whatever John St. Helen had done, or was running from, was his own affair. I was perfectly willing to accept his terms, as well as his dubious behavior. Especially as I truly came to know the man.

As I said before, St. Helen was a robust individual, and he cut quite the dashing figure. He was at least ten years my senior, in his late thirties, perhaps, with coal-black hair, deep-set dark eyes, and a flowing mustache. He was not overly-tall, but he was lean, and wiry. He walked with a pronounced limp, favoring his left leg, but the impediment did not detract from his bearing. He had a charismatic, almost theatrical flair about him, very confident and poised, with a quick wit and reckless charm that earned him an enviable favor with the ladies, and made his tiny tavern one of the most popular establishments in Glen Rose. He was well-educated, which was evident from his articulate speech, but he often seemed quite lackadaisical when it came to matters of business. He actually seemed more intent on entertaining his clientele than slaking their thirst. More than once I saw him leap upon his bar and render an ebullient, often brilliant oration from Shakespeare, or a poem by Tennyson, and it never seemed to bother him that his performance generally went unappreciated by his tipsy patrons. He was generous to a fault, flatly refusing to accept payment from any man who had worn the Rebel gray, which was fully two-thirds of the county. I often chided him that such benevolence would one day land him in the poorhouse. Yet he never seemed to lack for money, despite the fact that he lived in a squalid shack behind his tavern that would easily have put a Negro to shame. He never said where he was from, never once mentioned family or relatives, and, on those few occasions when we spoke together of serious matters, never alluded to any aspect of himself save for the present. But there were those rare times, when I would stop in after a long day in court, that John St. Helen would oddly let his guard down after several glasses of brandy, and I thought I could perceive a look of bleak despair gather within those piercing eyes. Here, I decided, was a man who had obviously lost all that was near and dear to him, and for whom sadness would undoubtedly remain a lifelong companion. I could not help but feel a certain sorrow for him.

St. Helen had up and sold his Glen Rose tavern, without explanation, and moved to Granbury about a year or so later. A mutual friend, F.J. Gordon, alluded to the fact that a young woman St. Helen was briefly involved with had become engaged to a federal marshal. St. Helen left Somervell County shortly before the wedding took place, whether out of fear or sadness no one knew. It was just another of the man's mysterious quirks, which Gordon and I tactfully chose to ignore. Gordon, who owned the Black Hawk Saloon, immediately offered St. Helen employment in his own establishment, and all of Granbury had welcomed the amiable barkeep with open arms. None more so than Mrs. Grady, whose husband had fallen alongside the city's namesake, General Hiram Granbury, on some blood-drenched Tennessee battlefield. I had never seen her so perky, nor as trusting, as when the handsome St. Helen had taken up residence under her roof. St. Helen himself seemed to develop an intimate, almost unique affection for the widow. And yet, curiously, it wasn't the least romantic.

I actually saw very little of St. Helen after his relocation, despite the fact that the Black Hawk was only a stone's throw from my door. My practice had grown considerably since the Unionists had been thrown out of Austin. Texas was finally beginning to recover from the carpetbaggers, and my clients included wealthy railroad entrepreneurs as well as penniless cowboys, in cases that ranged from mediation to murder. In dismal truth, St. Helen soon became just another name in a growing list of acquaintances. But then came Mrs. Grady's frantic note.

The sun had nearly set by the time I reached the big

Victorian house on Pearl Street. Lamps were already beginning to flicker behind the curtained windows, and the fading twilight cast shadows from the tall pecans over the long, rambling front porch. I hurried up the front steps and turned the bell key.

The widow Grady herself opened the front door. Elmira Grady was an attractive woman of only thirty-four, with auburn hair, sea-green eyes, and a buxom fullness that was not entirely unpleasing to the observer. I might even have been tempted to court her romantically myself, if it hadn't been for her three sons, undeniably the most reckless and malfeasant brats in all of Hood County. Some of their milder exploits included burglary and arson, yet the oldest was not quite twelve. How she managed to keep her boarders was anyone's guess, although I surmised the boys knew better than to practice their perfidies at home. More than once I had been called upon to rectify one or another such rascality, and I began to seriously wonder as to whether even my expertise might save them from an eventual trip to the gallows. Not that I was entirely certain I would want to.

I tugged off my dusty hat and managed a weary bow. "Good evening, Mrs. Grady."

The widow flashed a beaming Irish smile. "Mr. Bates! I'm so glad you got my note. I was beginning to think Billy might not have taken it round."

"Now why would you ever think something like that?" I asked with a smile of my own. "Might I come in, Mrs. Grady?"

She stepped partly aside. "Please. Let me take your things."

I shrugged out of my coat and glanced appraisingly around. She kept a clean and tidy house, despite the resident demons. I smiled again. "Your note sounded urgent."

The look in her green eyes suddenly turned anxious. "Oh, Mr. Bates, I fear it's truly dreadful! Mr. St. Helen is in a very bad way."

Suddenly I began to feel apprehensive, as though I should have taken the note far more seriously. I pointed a finger toward the ceiling. "Is he upstairs?"

"Yes. Dr. Ellis is with him." She shook her head, and I saw the tears begin to well. "He's been asking for you all afternoon, poor man. I do hope you've come in time."

"So do I," I said anxiously. "So do I." I turned and headed quickly for the stairs.

Dr. Bertram Ellis was coming out of St. Helen's room just as I reached the top. He nodded his bald head politely, gently closing the door behind him. "Bates. I see you finally made it."

"I've been in Glen Rose, Doctor Ellis. I would have come much sooner had I known." I glanced past him at the heavy oak door. "How is he?"

Dr. Ellis shrugged. "At death's door, if you ask him. He's even asked me to send for a priest."

"A priest?" I stared at him in puzzlement. "I didn't know he was Catholic."

"Apparently so. Unfortunately, the closest Papist church is in Fort Worth. I'll try and send off a telegram, but I truly don't think it's that serious."

"What's wrong with him?"

"Fever. Could be the ague, or possibly malaria. I asked him if he ever had it before, but he's not much for volunteering information." He gave me a frustrated scowl. "Perhaps you could manage to wheedle it out of him."

"I'll try. He doesn't always tell me much, either."

Ellis nodded curtly. "Well, in any event, I gave him a dose of quinine and some laudanum. I'll know better as to the prognosis in the morning." He set his leather satchel on a small hall table and took out a bottle of clear liquid. "Have Mrs. Grady give him a teaspoon of this every three hours. I'll be back to check on him first thing tomorrow."

"Can I go in?"

He snatched up his bag and waved it toward the door. "Please. You're all he's talked about since I've been here."

Ellis started down the stairs, and I reached out and turned the brass knob on St. Helen's door.

John St. Helen was propped up in bed, covered nearly to his chin with a heavy quilt despite the evening's balmy warmth. His dark hair was damp with sweat, plastered in curly ringlets against his forehead, and his entire face was pasty white. His eyes were closed as I entered, but they fluttered open with the sharp click of the latch.

"Finis," he smiled, and he tried to sit up. "Come in, Finis, please! I knew you wouldn't abandon your old friend!"

I rushed to his side, waving my hands frantically. "John, please! Don't try to move. Just lie still." He had reached out with one hand, and I took it immediately, blanching when I felt how cold and lifeless it seemed. "By God, John, you're as white as a ghost!"

He laughed at that, though weakly. "Indeed. And I fear I shall be one quite soon."

"Nonsense," I said, forcing a smile I did not feel. "Doctor Ellis says you'll be just fine."

St. Helen laughed again, falling back against his pillow. "A man of his calling could hardly say otherwise, could he? No, Finis, I fear this malady has me done for." His hand squeezed against mine, but I felt little strength behind it. "I'm just grateful that you were able to come in time." He nodded toward a chair next to the bed. "Sit down, Finis, please. There's something that I have to tell you."

"I wish you would save your strength, John," I insisted as I took the seat. "Whatever it is can wait until you're feeling better."

He shook his head slowly, and I could see that same tired

despair, as when we shared a drink, settle within his eyes. "No, I'm afraid it can't. Not anymore. Finis, I want you to know you're the only man I've ever been able to trust since I came to Texas. I know I've acted the fool, made a lot of people suspicious, but there was a reason. And you're the only person who never bothered to ask me what it was."

"I never felt it was any of my business," I told him honestly. "Part of being a lawyer, I suppose."

"No. Part of being a friend. You're a good man, Finis Bates. I mean that."

I squirmed in my seat, genuinely embarrassed. St. Helen caught my chagrin and laughed once more.

"Modesty hardly becomes a man like you, Finis. Do me a favor, will you? Reach in that drawer behind you and hand me that pouch."

I turned around and opened the chiffonier drawer he pointed to, passing over the leather bag that lay inside. Curious, I watched as St. Helen tugged at the drawstrings with trembling fingers. He reached in and pulled out a small, silver-framed tintype, which he stared at, quietly, for several pensive moments.

"This is a picture of my brother, Eddie," he said as he handed me the picture. "He lives in New York."

"His face is familiar," I mused as I frowned over the image. "Although I can't say why. I've never been to New York."

"He's an actor," St. Helen volunteered. "Quite talented, in fact. I want you to contact him, after I'm gone. I want him to know that I was still alive, at least for awhile."

I looked up at him curiously. "Still alive? You mean he thinks you're dead?"

"Many people think I'm dead. Which is why I am still alive."

I had to shake my head. "John, I'm sorry, but you have me

thoroughly confused. What is this all about?"

He turned to fix me with those dark eyes. "Finis, I have to tell you something, but I want you to promise me that it will never leave this room. Except for what you tell Eddie, you can never say anything to anyone else. Do you swear it?"

"I'm a lawyer, John, not a clergyman. But I'll keep your confidence as best I can. That I do promise."

"Fair enough," he sighed. He reached back into the pouch, then withdrew a second photograph. It was a cardboard *carte d'visite*, wrinkled and torn, showing a dark-haired, dashingly handsome young man poised dramatically against a theatrical background. He held it out to me. "Do you know who that is?"

"It looks very much like you," I said with a shrug. "Though much younger."

"The fellow's name is on the back," he said flatly.

I took the faded paper and flipped it around. For several long moments, I could only gape at the penciled words. Slowly, I lifted my disbelieving eyes to St. Helen's.

"The evil that men do lives after them," he said with a mournful smile. "Shakespeare, dear Finis. The most consummate judge of the human character the world has ever known." He waved a weary hand toward the photograph. "Yes, it is me. And I was much younger, then. And far more foolish. That's the secret, Finis, the one you've never tried to discern. The one that I've never revealed to another living soul. You see, I am not John St. Helen. My name, my real name, is John Wilkes Booth . . ."

Chapter Two

Finish, good lady, the bright day is done,
And we are done for the dark.
　　　　　---Antony and Cleopatra---

Washington, D.C. - April, 1865

It was over, finished, the entire Cause was lost. I stood at the window of my room, there in the National Hotel, and I watched as the world came to an insidious end.

Word of Lee's surrender had roared through Washington City on demon's wings, and the mad fools below had wasted no time in celebrating. Men, women, and even children filled the square at Sixth and Pennsylvania, leaping and dancing about like lunatics loosed from an asylum. And the Negroes were among them, of course. The black monkeys congregated on every corner and chittered Lincoln's filthy name, over and over again, until it sounded for all the world like the call of some garrulous bird. Somewhere a band played, adding to the hideous din, and the fools even launched fireworks over the Capitol dome. As I watched, a single rocket broke away from its normal trajectory, hissing through the night sky until it exploded almost directly above the monster's den known as the White House. I found myself wishing, as the shower of brilliant sparks slowly settled around Old Abe, that they might really have been Confederate shells. The Original Gorilla was undoubtedly sharing the same sight, with a smile of triumph, no doubt, and the very thought, of his ugly, grinning face, made the humiliation that much worse. I threw the window shut and slammed my fist against the sill, and for the first time in my life I truly understood the Mad Dane's terrible anguish. Oh, that this too, too solid flesh would melt . . . .

"Johnny, are you all right?"

The girl's voice startled me, and I nearly leapt out of my skin. "Oh, yes, I'm quite fine, Prudy," I snarled over my shoulder. "I'm merely watching the world go to hell."

She laughed at that—laughed—as though it were actually funny. "Oh, Johnny, really . . ." I heard her slip out of bed and pad across the wooden floor, then I felt her soft, naked breasts press warmly against my back. "Don't be like that, not tonight." Her hands slipped around my waist and began a slow descent. "Please?"

I nudged her away, somewhat roughly. "Prudy, go away. I'm not in the mood anymore."

"Really?" She pressed against me once again, and I felt the flick of her tongue across my shoulder. "You certainly were earlier, Johnny sweet. Perhaps I can change your mind?"

I started to push her away again, but for some reason, I decided to leave her hands to their skillful wandering. Despite my melancholia, I could not easily turn her away. Prudy was, without question, a delightful little tart. Prudence Elizabeth Carlysle, a nubile, green-eyed blond nymph, from one of the more genteel families of Baltimore. Or perhaps it was Annapolis. I couldn't remember. She was a most intriguing young woman, no stranger to Washington's most elite social circles. Or it's most prominent bedrooms. Yet she was barely twenty-two years old. She fancied herself an actress, and currently had a bit part in Our American Cousin, Laura Keene's pet project that had been playing down at Ford's for what seemed like a millennium. That was where I had met her, back in far better days. Prudy had indeed displayed a modicum of talent, those few times I had seen her act. But by far and away, her best performances were in bed. On that stage, Prudence Carlysle had absolutely no peer.

She had shown up at my door shortly after sunset, drunk

with champagne and wanting a tumble. I was hardly in the amorous mood, having just returned from a turbulent visit with my brother Edwin in Boston, only to learn that the South had fallen. My first inclination was to send her packing, and then to drown myself in a dozen bottles of brandy. But Prudy was impossible to resist, especially as she'd been virtually naked beneath her cloak, and I had obliged her, though more as a means to vent my frustrated rage than to satiate desire. Not that it mattered one whit to my little actress.

Her fingers now played a particularly impressive role. "There now," she whispered against my neck. "Doesn't that feel good, Johnny sweet? Tell me, can your beloved Bessie do that?"

For several luxurious moments, I forgot what was occurring beyond the window. "My beloved Bessie," I managed to sigh, "hasn't the slightest knowledge of such wicked diversions."

Prudy giggled mischievously. "But Johnny, she's your fiancee."

It was my turn to laugh. "Our betrothal is slightly more show than substance, my dear. Unlike yours, Bessie's virtue proved a far more formidable bastion to my usual assaults. Even my poetry was ineffective."

"So you proposed marriage instead?" Prudy's laughter became nearly uncontrollable. "How delicious! But what about Senator Hale? Won't he be furious when he learns his daughter's precious innocence has been betrayed? And by the lecherous Johnny Booth, no less?"

"I hardly think he'll even notice. The drunken sot can barely remember his own name, half the time. Besides, he's been appointed ambassador to Spain. He's leaving in June, and Bessie's agreed to go with him, at least for a few months. We've agreed to postpone any firm commitment till after she's returned."

"And by then you'll be conveniently on theatrical tour,"

Prudy concluded, once more plying her wondrous dexterity. "Oh, Johnny, how wonderfully devious you are!" She kissed the back of my neck, then traced a curious finger along a rough, raised line of flesh beneath my ear. "Tell me, Johnny sweet, did you really get this scar in a duel over a lady's honor?"

I glanced back at her, feigning an indignant scowl. "You find that difficult to believe?"

"I do," she said sweetly. "The ladies you know have no honor. Not for long, that is."

"Ah, but they lose it ever so gratefully," I laughed, turning around to pull her close. I slipped my hands around her exquisite buttocks. "Just as you did, Prudy dear."

She gave me an impish grin, through a tangled cascade of long blonde hair. "I'm afraid that wasn't your conquest, Johnny sweet. So how did you get the scar?"

I shrugged. "Alas, just a lowly carbuncle. The surgeon's incision opened during a play, when I was grappling with Charlotte Cushman. But a lady was involved, so I suppose you could say it's half true."

"I wouldn't care if it was a lie," Prudy sighed. She laid her head against my chest. "I wouldn't care if everything you said were all lies, Johnny Booth. I'd still love you as much as I do now."

I pushed her to arm's length, frowning at her sharply. "Prudy, don't—"

"Ooh!" Prudy suddenly squealed with delight, as another skyrocket exploded, bathing the room, and our naked bodies, in a garish red light. "Fireworks! I love fireworks! Don't you love fireworks, Johnny?"

It was then that my depression, as well as my anger, returned with a vengeance. "I'd prefer them to be Confederate carronades!"

"Honestly, Johnny!" Prudy pulled away to slap irritably at

my shoulder. "What's wrong with you? I'd think you could at least be happy tonight, of all nights. After all, the war is over."

"It isn't over, it's lost!" There was a bottle of Napolean brandy, my favorite comfort and balm, on the table near the bed. I swiftly snatched it up and pulled the cork, then drained a third of the contents in a single furious gulp. "Everything I ever believed in is lost. Though I suppose a brainless little whore like yourself couldn't possibly understand that."

Her lithe body stiffened in the dim light. "I'm not a whore," she said finally, in a very small, very quavering voice. "And I'm not brainless, either. You shouldn't say things like that, Johnny." She turned up a lamp on the table, and I caught the glimmer of a tear in her eye as she started to get dressed. "I know where your sympathies lie. All of Washington knows it, for God's sake! It just seems to me you'd take heart in the fact that the killing is finally over."

I glared at her contemptuously. "What would you know about it, Prudy? What would you know about killing and war, or a cause you've devoted your entire life to?"

"Cause?" Prudy worked angry fingers at the buttons of her lace camisole, pausing long enough to cast me a cold, sardonic scowl. "What cause are you referring to, Johnny? The only cause you've ever been devoted to was your own vanity. And God help whatever man, woman, or country that ever stood in the way of that noble effort!"

Something inside of me seemed to explode, just like one of those damnable skyrockets. I stepped forward and slapped her, hard, and she fell back across the bed with a horrified yelp.

I stood over her with my hands clenched in trembling fists. "You contemptible little bitch! Who the hell do you think you are? Don't ever presume you know me! No one knows John Wilkes Booth! No one!"

She rubbed at her face, finally losing the struggle to hold

back tears. "You had no right to hit me, Johnny."

Seething, I slowly moved towards her. "Oh, I'll do more than just hit you, Prudy dear. I'll make goddamned certain you never forget a single word I said!"

There was an almost animal terror on her face as I fell on top of her, and indeed, she fought me like a lynx in a trap. But I was far too strong, and the noise from outside more than sufficient to muffle her screams. I had never taken a woman by force, not like that, and I suppose there was a part of me that cringed in shame even as I raped her. But it was almost as if Prudy herself did not exist. I was aware of her piteous cries, I felt her desperate struggles beneath me, yet it was more as though she had somehow become the very embodiment of everything I hated, and feared. Her words, which still rang in my ears despite the thunderous explosions outside, had come far too close to the truth. A truth which I could not bring myself to admit.

How long I assailed her I don't remember, but it was only after she went completely limp beneath me that I finally pulled away. I stumbled away from the bed, covering my face with my hands at the sight of my depravity. "Oh, Christ! Prudy, I don't . . . I can't . . . Jesus, what have I done?"

Prudy rolled over, twisting and groaning in pain. "Oh, God, Johnny, you hurt me so bad!" Her voice was muffled by a pillow, but there was no mistaking her anguish. "Why did you hurt me so bad?"

I staggered to the window, staring down numbly at the crowd of cretins who, if anything, had doubled in size and gaiety since the night began. The sound of their laughter mingled with Prudy's terrible sobs, and I couldn't stand it. Not any longer. A drawer in the table held a LeMat revolver, and I tugged it open, staring wistfully down at the cold blue steel as if greeting a welcome friend. I reached out for it, fully intending to put it against my temple, but my hand suddenly pulled away before my fingers could even brush the ivory grips. I fell back against the wall, shivering in rage and despair. Lost. Everything, including my own nerve, was lost forever . . . .

"Get out, Johnny," Prudy suddenly said. "I don't ever want to see you again!"

I turned around, sighing. "Prudy, please, I'm sorry! I didn't mean—"

"Get out!" she hissed again. She sat up, anxiously fumbling for a beaded handbag that sat on the little stand next to the bed. A small, gleaming object suddenly appeared in one hand, and I found myself staring into the tiny black eye of a derringer. "I'll kill you, Johnny," she snarled above the gun. "So help me God I will!"

Slowly, I stepped towards her. The gun never wavered, nor did the murderous look of hatred that twisted Prudy's angelic face. "Go ahead, Prudy," I said ruefully. "Shoot me." My eyes locked with hers, and I tapped at my forehead. "Right here."

She hesitated, beautiful lips quivering in silent, tearful fury as her knuckles went white around the gun. I leaned forward, nearly in tears myself.

"What are you waiting for?" I grabbed her arm, pressing the gun against my head. "Kill me, goddamn it! I can't do it myself! For God's sake, Prudy, I have nothing left to live for! Please," I begged pleadingly. "Kill me . . ."

I heard the hammer click; a glorious, magnificent sound. Arms against a sea of troubles. I drew in my breath, closing my eyes gratefully as I braced myself for the shot.

It never came.

"I can't," Prudy sobbed. I opened my eyes to see her lying back against the headboard, staring at me with eyes that burned with both sorrow and betrayal. She tossed the gun into the rumpled bedclothes. "I hate you with all my soul, Johnny Booth, but I love you just as much. Just go away and leave me alone."

I picked up the gun, staring bleakly at the ugly, blunt lines and tarnished steel. "Thus conscience doth make cowards of us all."

"What did you say?"

I shook my head slowly, handing back the gun. "Nothing."

Prudy waved it away angrily. "Keep it, Johnny. Who knows? Maybe you'll find the courage to use it on yourself."

A mutual wish, I wanted desperately to say. But I kept my dismal silence, picking up my waistcoat to shove the derringer into a pocket. "You can stay here if you want, Prudy," I said as I started to get dressed. "I'll take a room at the Kirkwood."

She looked away, but I caught the painful wince. "Please, Johnny, spare me your hollow pity. I want nothing more from you, ever. I'll be gone before morning. I just need to rest awhile." She curled up on the bed and started to cry again, this time more softly.

I stared at her silently, unable to find words that matched my tumultuous emotions, then shrugged into my coat, turned down the lamp, and started to leave.

"Someday you won't be so lucky, Johnny," Prudy called out suddenly. "Someday someone will actually have the nerve to kill you."

My hand paused on the latch. "I have no doubts you are right, Prudy. But I truly wish to God it might have been you. You would have been doing us both a favor."

I opened the door and stepped out, leaving her to cry in the dark.

Chapter Three

Of comfort no man speak;
Let us talk of graves, of worms, and epitaphs . . .
~~~Richard II~~~

I made my way out of the National by way of the back stairs, hoping to avoid the teeming madness on Sixth Street. The alley behind the hotel reeked of urine and all manner of offal, but in truth I did not care. The foul stench matched my mood. My head still rang with Prudy's sobs, and I could not erase the wretched sight of her lying so helplessly on my bed. It was not within me to behave so cruelly, so wantonly, yet I had done so without thought or care. But much about me was suddenly no longer familiar.

There were but a few drunks and merrymakers in the alleys as I hurried through the balmy night. Most were too deeply immersed in their cups to notice me, although I was wearing my best silk coat and diamond stickpin, and surely presented a tempting sight to any ruffian. But my visage, within the dim lantern light that filtered from nearby windows, must have been equally portentous, for, while one or two burly fellows did stumble in my direction, they just as swiftly reeled away when I coldly met their bloodshot eyes. And the sight of a bone-handled dagger, which I always kept sheathed beneath my cloak, undoubtedly assisted in the persuasion.

But the alleys could not mute the night's bacchanal air, and I found myself thinking, as I trudged through the muck, how much Edwin would have enjoyed these festivities. He was a staunch Unionist, my brother, and our parting words, as I'd left him in Boston only a few days before, had not been the least pleasant. The war had been the sole issue that held the two of us so fiercely at odds. Yet it seemed almost preordained that such division would exist, given the very nature of our locales. Edwin was the toast of Broadway, the darling of the North, while I was more popular in the South. And our older brother, and our father's namesake, Junius, held sway over his own audiences in the far western realm of San Francisco. It was said, and not without some veracity, that the Booth brothers were as diverse as America itself.

Edwin and I had tried to put our political differences aside, and had even appeared together, along with Junius, in a benefit production of Julius Caesar less than five months before in New York City. But that selfsame night, as Edwin's Brutus was denounced by my Antony, a band of Confederate loyalists set a series of fires across Manhattan. Backstage, I had praised their heroic efforts, angrily reminding Edwin of the conflagrations that had consumed Atlanta and the Shenandoah Valley. But, as was usual, my brother had only contempt for all things Southern. Even Junius, who proudly boasted of his affiliation with the San Francisco Vigilance Committee, had voiced his fervent hope that the saboteurs might be hanged. Critically, our performance that night was considered a triumph. Privately, I could not wait to return south. And I doubted sincerely that the Booth brothers would ever perform together again.

I stepped out of the alley at E Street, and for a moment or two stood pondering my next course. A group of Negro soldiers huddled on the corner, glibly warbling some insipid tune about "freedom" and "Moses", and I had to look fumingly away. The sight of those jackanapes in that uniform was enough to make my blood boil. I hurried across the street, ignoring a teamster's angry curse as I raced in front of his team. It was much more preferable, as far as I was concerned, to be run down by a beer wagon than face such a damnable disgrace.

I thought about heading north, to H Street and Widow

Surratt's, then swiftly, and dejectedly, thought the better of it. I wasn't up to facing John and the others tonight, kindred spirits though they were. Whatever schemes we might have fashioned, no matter how bold or decisive, were absolutely futile now. And it did no good to dwell on what could never be. Cursing under my breath, I turned and headed west.

Chris Made's Grand Saloon, at the corner of Tenth and E, was alive with light and sound. Yet I passed on by, scowling at the raucous laughter, and a few steps later, found myself outside of Volkner's. The sounds that emanated from within were far more subdued, so I took a chance and slipped inside.

Volkner's was what the fine ladies of Washington society sneeringly referred to as lowbrow; meaning that it was frequented by the common working man. It was run by the widow of its original owner, Hans Volkner, who had tied on her husband's stained apron when Hans died of smallpox barely a year after arriving in America. Unlike the Grand, where one was apt to find gold-braided military officers and silk-suited Congressmen, Widow Volkner's clientele were far less dignified, and included mechanics, teamsters, stagehands, and other such nefarious riffraff. Yet I found myself far more relaxed and lethargic within its filthy, tar-papered walls than among the polished brass and red-carpeted finery of the Grand. It was, at least to my way of thinking, the same sort of retreat my father would have sought for himself. Junius Brutus Booth had been a man of the streets, rising from the very gutters of London to become the most popular actor in both England and America. Yet he never once forgot his origins. These selfsame commoners, lowbrows, and castoffs had been his people, and now they were mine.

Volkner's atmosphere was as sullen as the smoky lantern light that barely illuminated the cramped interior. Many of the widow's patrons were Southern sympathizers, another reason I found solace within, and like myself, they had very little reason for rejoicing this bitter night. A handful of Union soldiers, cavalrymen, by their muddy boots, raised their glasses in chortling toasts in a dim corner. But the vast majority of customers, hunched over rickety tables or huddled around the dilapidated bar, kept their conversations to a glum murmur.

A few looked up as I entered, and I suddenly heard my name called eagerly.

"Johnny!"

"Wilkes Booth, you rascal! Where the hell have you been?"

"Come on in, John! Come drown your sorrows with us!"

I waved my walking stick in a weary acknowledgment. "Greetings to you all, gentlemen." I flicked a wary glance towards the Yankee horsemen. "Though I wish they might be given under more joyous circumstances." I walked up to the bar and tossed several coins on the gouged and warped oak surface. "A bottle of your best, Carl. Let me know when that runs out, and I'll happily replace it."

Carl Gustav, Hannah Volkner's brother and sometimes barkeep, scooped up the money in a huge hand and loosed a beer-scented guffaw. He flashed a broken-toothed smile beneath his bushy mustache. "Don't you worry, Mr. Booth. I don't let you go thirsty." He reached under the bar and set a bottle of brandy before me. True to form, he offered no glass.

"Where is Widow Volkner tonight?" I asked as I pulled the cork.

Carl pointed over his bald head. "Upstairs. I tell her you're here, Mr. Booth."

I shook my head quickly. "Don't disturb her. I'm afraid I'm not fit company tonight." I turned and headed towards an empty table in a far corner.

"Say, Wilkes," someone called. "How about a verse?"

Several others echoed the request, but I waved them off. "Gentlemen, please, not tonight. Normally I would love to accommodate you, but I'm simply not in the mood." I studied each face somberly. "Surely you can understand."

"Just one verse, Mr. Booth?" A thin young man, whom I knew to be a prompter over at Grover's Theater, as well as a fellow Southerner, touched me gently on the shoulder. "Please?"

I started to object, then caught the dismal glimmer in his dark eyes, undoubtedly a twin to my own. "All right," I nodded at length. "But just one."

The barroom went silent, as every man's eye turned towards me. Even the soldiers were watching with curious frowns. I drew in my breath and lifted my gaze to the soot-stained rafters.

"Come not, when I am dead,
To shed thy tears around my head,
Let the wind weep, and the plover cry,
But thou, oh fool man, pass by . . ."

I lowered my eyes to the cheerless stares around me. "Tennyson," I smiled, slowly raising the bottle. "To the Confederacy, dear friends. God grant she may never be forgotten."

"To the Confederacy!" several toasted mournfully. The cavalrymen glanced angrily at one another, then at me, but apparently felt themselves sufficiently outnumbered. They swiftly drained their glasses and hurried out.

I continued on through the bar, nodding quietly at the countless backslaps and mumbled compliments. I sat down at the little table, with my back to the wall, and gulped down what I hoped would be the first of many welcome swigs. Something gouged against my hip, as I leaned back in the chair, and I dug through my coat pocket and pulled out the little derringer I had taken from Prudy.

It was an odd-looking little gun. A Brown, according to the letters etched under the barrel, though I had never heard of that particular gunsmith. The two-inch barrel swiveled sideways, when I pressed a tiny lever, revealing a single brass cartridge in the breech. I tugged out the bullet, frowning over the lead projectile which, only a short while before, I had wanted so desperately put through my skull. It was not yet too late, I sighed to myself. I reloaded the gun, then held it cradled in both hands, lost in a sea of anxious and troubled thoughts.

"Planning to kill someone, Johnny?"

I snapped out of my reverie, glancing up to meet the smiling but wary eyes of the Widow Volkner.

"Not really." I forced my own smile as I quickly pocketed the gun. "No one of importance, anyway."

"Good," she nodded. "Too much killing already, *ja*?" She waved at one of the chairs. "Mind if I sit down?"

I stood up, offering my most gracious bow. "I insist upon it, Widow Volkner."

She laughed as she settled into a rickety chair. "Ach, Widow Volkner, is it? *Mein Gott,* Johnny, I am not old lady!" She studied me silently, appraisingly. "Not that old, anyway."

I had to laugh. Hannah Volkner was nearly fifty, but in truth, she was still quite comely for her age. Her hair was the color of woven flax, with more than a trace of silver, but she always wore it braided, in the fashion of her native Bavaria. Her eyes were dark blue, and her full mouth had but a few unsightly wrinkles tugging at the sides. Her figure was not quite so youthful, confined as it was beneath a tight corset and a heavy green muslin dress, yet I could not help but believe Hannah had been a most desirable woman merely a few short years before. And, much to my own surprise, I found myself wondering what it might have been like to bed her, given that she was nearly twice my age. I had tumbled with a number of women, to be certain, but none beyond the age of forty. But it was still most provocative.

Hannah must have caught the speculative gleam in my eye,

for I saw her blush slightly and turn her eyes away. "You don't come here so much anymore, Johnny," she said quickly. "Not since last month, *ja?*"

"I've been away," I shrugged, taking another deep drink. "I had to travel north for a few weeks, on business."

Her indigo eyes widened eagerly. "You are in a play, *ja?* The Marble Heart, maybe?" She gave me a broad, genuinely adoring smile. "That one is my favorite, Johnny. You are so good in that one." She put her hand against her ample bosom, and I actually saw tears begin to well. "When you carve the statues, and they come to life, it is so beautiful it nearly breaks my heart!"

"No, I wasn't in a play, Hannah. To be honest, I haven't been on the stage for some time now. I was visiting my brother Edwin. And I have some money invested in oil leases, in Pennsylvania and Canada."

She frowned at me in bewilderment. "Oil? What you want with oil, Johnny? You are an actor, *ja?* You belong on the stage." She slipped a warm hand over mine. "So tell me, when does Hannah come to see you act again?"

This time it was my turn to look away. "I don't know, Hannah. I truly don't. I've had trouble with bronchitis this past winter. My stage voice isn't what it should be. I've been hoping the time I've spent away from the theater might have helped, but I seem to stay hoarse almost constantly." I gave her a reassuring wink. "Perhaps in another month or so I'll be back in top form."

"You will invite Hannah to your performance, *ja?*"

"I promise you'll have a front row seat."

"Good!" She squeezed my hand affectionately and stood up. "I must go back upstairs, Johnny. I have ledgers to balance, *ja?* Carl tells me you are here, but I can only say hello." She bent down and gave me a gentle, motherly, yet somehow, extremely enticing kiss. "Perhaps you come back sometime later, *ja?*"

I smiled up at her. "Perhaps."

She turned and quickly disappeared through a narrow doorway near the bar. I stared after her for a moment, frowning speculatively to myself, then quickly shook my head in chagrin and turned my attention back to my rapidly emptying bottle. I waved at Carl, who nodded when I tapped the amber glass. That's when I noticed the tall, bearded man who stood at the bar, staring directly at me with a look of unbridled contempt. He wore a dark suit of a rather common cut, but there was something about his bearing, like the squared shoulders and coiled-spring stance, that suggested he usually wore a uniform. A blue uniform.

I held his cold stare for several moments, breaking with his dark eyes only when Carl brought me another bottle. Yet they were waiting when I glanced back, with the same stark, malevolent glare. I began to feel exceedingly unnerved. He hadn't been in Volkner's when I had arrived, and I hadn't seen him come in. Nor did I have the slightest idea as to who he might have been. He held a drink in his left hand, while the right rested against his hip, just inches away from a Colt revolver tucked into his trousers. He saw me glance at the gun and he smiled; a thin, evil little curl of his lips beneath the thick beard. I took another pull at the brandy and swiftly, anxiously, forced my gaze away.

The front door banged open suddenly, and a very stout, very drunk little man reeled into the barroom, waving a miniature Union flag with tremendous glee.

"God bless America!" he shouted jubilantly. "God bless President Lincoln!"

Several men fairly leaped out of their chairs, swiftly surrounding the drunken fool like a pack of snarling wolves. He fought at them, thoroughly confused, flailing his thick arms and screeching wildly. They had nearly forced him to the door by the time I made it across the room.

"Let him go!" I shouted above the din. I pulled two of the attackers away, then brandished my cane at the rest. "Let him go, damn it!"

They gaped at me in confusion, but they let go the drunk.

"But Mr. Booth," the young prompter from Grover's pleaded. "Didn't you hear what he said?"

"I heard," I said curtly. "But we are Southern gentlemen, not Yankee hooligans." I turned to the fat man, who was indignantly brushing himself off, glaring about through bloodshot and totally befuddled eyes. "Sir," I said to him calmly, "that name is neither mentioned nor welcomed in this establishment."

"Wha . . . ?" He tried, unsuccessfully, to focus his angry stare on me. "What are you talking about? What name?"

I forced myself to hiss the word. "Lincoln."

He started at that, mouth falling agape. "But . . . but, he's our president, for God's sake!"

"He may be your president, but he is most assuredly not mine. I have no use whatsoever for the likes of King Abraham." I waved the cane towards the door. "Please take your exuberance elsewhere."

He finally understood what was occurring. "Copperheads," he snarled furiously. "Goddamn treasonous copperheads!" He shook a pudgy finger at the glowering faces that surrounded him. "They ought to hang the lot of you bastards!"

I gave him a mocking smile. "Be that as it may, the fact remains that you are still unwanted here. And a man of your considerable bulk shouldn't tarry where he isn't wanted." I nodded at the others. "I can't promise how long I might be able to restrain my companions."

He stumbled forward, frowning curiously as he studied my face. "Say, don't I know you? Where have I seen you before?"

I drew myself up, proudly. "My name is John Wilkes

Booth."

"Booth? The actor? Son of a bitch!" He shook his head in open disgust. "I never would have taken you for a traitor!" He reached down and picked up his fallen flag, then headed for the door. He stopped, suddenly, turning to spit on the floor. "That's what I think of you secesh bastards! I hope they hang Jeff Davis! And Bobby Lee!" The door slammed sharply behind him.

"You should've let us have him, Mr. Booth," the young prompter said bitterly. "We'd've taught him a thing or two about the South."

I shook my head. "The fat slob wasn't worth it. No Yankee's worth it." I suddenly thought about the bearded man, and I glanced around the barroom quickly. He was nowhere in sight. I looked at Carl Gustav. "Carl, what happened to that tall fellow, the one who was standing by the bar?"

"He leave out the back," the barkeep replied, jerking a thumb over his shoulder. "You know him, Mr. Booth?"

"No. I never saw him before."

"He knew you," Carl insisted. "Said to tell you he'd see you again, and for you to say hello to Mr. Surratt and Mr. Paine. You know those names, Mr. Booth? Mr. Booth . . . ?"

"What?" I suddenly regained my composure. "Ah, yes, yes of course! His name must have slipped my mind for a moment. I remember who he is, now." I dug into my pockets, trying to force my hands to stop their desperate trembling. I peeled off several notes from a thick wad of currency, flashing my broadest smile to the barroom. "Gentlemen, I'm afraid I'm too fatigued to linger with you any longer. But please, enjoy what little comfort you might on Wilkes Booth."

There was a chorus of gratitude as I threw the money on the bar and hurriedly made my way to the door.

"How about another verse, John?"

I stopped, turning to shake my head. "No, gentlemen, no

more verses." I smiled my good-byes and swiftly stepped outside, where I barely managed to stumble into a nearby alley before I was violently sick.

I pressed my hands against a nearby wall for support, shivering in a night that was not cold. "No more verses," I heard myself rasp. "No more life . . ."

Chapter Four

O conspiracy,
Shan'st thou show thy dangerous brow by night,
When evils are most free.
       ~~~Julius Caesar~~~

I do not remember how I returned to the National. I may have run the entire distance, for when I finally snapped out of my terrified daze, my heart was racing and my head fairly pounding with pain, and I found myself leaning against one of the tall stone columns that graced the hotel's front entrance. The night's wretched hoopla had not decreased, yet only a few curious heads bothered to turn in my direction. To them I was but another drunken reveler, and for once in my life, I was actually grateful for the anonymity. Had anyone bothered to peer more closely into my face, pressed ever so tightly against the cold granite, they would have seen the mortal fear that was surely etched there.

I had to leave Washington City, perhaps even America itself, this very night. Whoever the tall stranger had been, whatever his vile intent in Volkner's, he had known of names that were best left unknown, at least among those who were not allies. And in that knowledge was sealed my very doom. I had not the slightest idea where to run, save to Canada, where I knew several loyal Confederates who had already found refuge. Or perhaps to my father's homeland, once valiantly dedicated to our noble Cause. But in truth, it did not overly matter. I no longer had a country, and that which might lay claim to me now offered only a hangman's noose. A noose I could actually feel tightening with every gasping breath.

I summoned up what courage I could and hurried inside the hotel, ignoring the startled gape of the red-coated doorman when he recognized the staggering derelict. The huge, ornate lobby was ablaze with light, and gay music wafted through the open doors of the nearby ballroom. Yet my troubled thoughts were hardly focused on the silk suits and ruffled taffeta that whirled within, nor on the anxious face of young Merrick, the desk clerk, who waved at me quite ardently as I started up the carpeted stairs. He may have even called my name, but I could hear only my own heartbeat, and, oddly enough, the desperate words from the Scottish Play that my father was always loathe to perform. Let us not be dainty about leave-taking, but whift away . . .

I fumbled in my pockets for the key, as I rounded the second-floor landing. But as I approached room 228, I suddenly noticed that the door was slightly ajar. I slipped my right hand into my coat pocket, closing a nervous hand around the tiny derringer, then used my cane to slowly, warily, push in the door. All was black within the room, and the dim light from the corridor lamps revealed a small, motionless silhouette perched upon the bed.

"Prudy," I smiled, with a genuine sigh of relief. "I'm so glad you decided to—"

The fist caught me full in the stomach, and I doubled over in horrific pain, just as another iron blow hammered down on the back of my neck and sent me gasping to the floor. I heard the door slam shut, as a heavy boot swiftly pressed down on my left wrist, and I felt the walking stick kicked from my grasp. A pair of none-too-gentle hands yanked my right hand away from my side and quickly rummaged through my clothes. I could not speak, so great was the agony, and the only light I could perceive were the flashing stars of pain that danced before my terrified eyes.

"He has a pistol," I heard a deep voice rumble above me. "And this dagger."

"Throw them on the bed," another man snarled. "Make

certain that's all he's carrying."

I felt my pockets turned inside-out. "Nothing else, save for his money." There was a low, grudging whistle. "Hardly destitute, is he?"

"Of course not," a third voice suddenly joined in, and the tone was almost jovial. "Mr. Booth is a man of considerable means. I understand he earns nearly twenty thousand dollars per year. More than the vice-president, in fact. Please lift him to his feet, gentlemen."

Twin pairs of hands hauled me up from the carpet and held me in a vise-like grip. I shook my head to try and clear away the foggy pain, then peered through the darkness at the blurry shadow that slowly detached itself from the bed and crossed the room. A match suddenly flared; a brilliant flash that caused me to blink, and then the kerosene lamp on the table was turned up.

"Who . . . who are you?" I managed to rasp. "What are you doing here?"

The flickering light revealed a short, pudgy, middle-aged man with thinning dark hair, gold-rimmed spectacles, and thick, flowing chin whiskers streaked with gray. He studied me, quite intently, peering over the top of his glasses. "Don't you know who I am, Mr. Booth?"

In truth, he did look familiar, but I was in no condition to remember his name. I forced a contemptuous smile, summoning a bravado that I most assuredly did not feel. "Judging from the cut of your suit, I'd say you were a goddamned Yankee bureaucrat."

My right arm was suddenly, painfully, twisted behind my back. "Rebel pig!" a voice hissed in my ear. "You watch your mouth!"

"Enough, lieutenant." The pudgy man held up a small hand, shaking his head rapidly. "There's no need for violence. Mr. Booth's insults are of little consequence. Please find him a chair, if you would. We may be here for some time, and I don't wish him to think us inhospitable."

My captors tugged me backwards and pushed me down into an armchair.

"Shall we bind him, sir?" one of them asked.

The pudgy man shook his head again. "He's not going anywhere, gentlemen. You can let go of him."

The two men released my arms and stepped cautiously away from the chair. I turned to glare at both. One was of medium height, with curly dark hair and a thin mustache. He wore the dark blue uniform of an infantry colonel, along with a holstered revolver, which he drew now and leveled at me as he took a wary stance by the door. I slid a contemptuous scowl from him to the second man, and suddenly started.

It was the tall bastard from Volkner's.

"You!" I rasped, rising out of the chair. His pistol was in my face before I could straighten up.

"Please sit down, Mr. Booth," the pudgy man sighed. "It is in your best interest to remain completely calm."

I dropped back into the chair, but my eyes never left the tall man, who only grinned malevolently at me above the gun. I forced my glare back to the pudgy man. "Will someone please tell me what the hell this is all about?"

"Allow me to introduce my associates. The gentleman in uniform is Colonel Lafayette Baker, chief of detectives for the United States' Secret Service. This other gentleman, whom you've undoubtedly seen before, is Lieutenant Luther Baker, the colonel's cousin."

I had to swallow the burning bile in my throat. "And you are . . . ?"

"My name is Edwin Stanton, Mr. Booth. United States' Secretary of War."

"Jesus Almighty Christ . . ." I felt the breath leave my body in a single tremulous gasp. Edwin Stanton, Abraham

Lincoln's iron right fist. Imprisoner, inquisitor, and usurper of Constitutional rights. A man who was hated by every southern loyalist as intensely as Lincoln himself, yet doubly feared. A man who was rumored to keep the moldering body of a dead child in a box beneath his bed. A man who held the power of life and death over thousands in those small, neatly manicured hands . . .

And a man who was now standing less than an arm's length before me.

I met his placid eyes with my own transfixed gape, and I realized, like Caesar before Brutus, that I was staring at my own executioner.

A thousand frantic thoughts began to race through my mind, as I desperately sought a means of escape. I glanced past Stanton, at the little derringer which lay only a few feet away on the bedside table. Yet the pistol would provide only a single shot, and there were twin Colts staring me down. I flicked my eyes instead to the window, less than ten feet away, and swiftly calculated the distance to the street below.

Stanton apparently read my anxious thoughts, for he shook his head with a thin, almost sardonic smile. "Don't be foolish, Mr. Booth. While I realize you are quite renowned for your theatrical agility, this is hardly a stage." He pulled out a chair from the table and sat down. "And it is most assuredly not a play."

I sat back in my own chair, drawing upon everything within me to remain as stoic as possible. It might not have been a play, as he so snidely insisted, but I was still a consummate actor, and I would not give the Yankee bastard the pleasure of watching me grovel. I crossed my legs coolly, smiling at him over the tips of steepled fingers.

"Indeed it is not, Mr. Secretary. But neither is it clear to me as to your reasons for being here. Are you and your . . ." I glanced coldly at the two Bakers, "associates . . . in the habit of waylaying innocent citizens in their hotel rooms?"

Stanton held my eyes with an angry glare, the first emotion I had seen him display. "No, Mr. Booth, I can safely assure you we are not in the habit of waylaying anyone who is innocent."

"Then perhaps you'd care to explain this invasion of my privacy. Or is it just another example of Yankee despotism?"

Stanton beckoned to Col. Baker. "Colonel, perhaps you should sit down here and explain the situation to Mr. Booth, since you are far more familiar with the particulars."

The officer holstered his gun and crossed the room, pulling a thin notebook from within his blouse as he sat down opposite Stanton. Luther Baker quickly took his cousin's place at the door, never once turning the Colt's muzzle from my head.

Col. Baker flipped the notebook open. "John Wilkes Booth," he began, fixing me with a sullen, almost laconic frown as he thumbed through the pages. "Born in Bel Air, Maryland, May tenth, eighteen thirty-eight. Third son of noted actor Junius Brutus Booth—"

"Fifth," I said tersely.

He looked up at me, puzzled. "How's that?"

"I am Junius Booth's fifth son, not his third. Two of my older brothers died in youth."

He seemed annoyed at that, which actually pleased me. "Hardly significant," I heard him mumble, yet he made a penciled notation before he continued. "Actor of some renown, yet often criticized for bombastic and overly dramatic performances—"

"Bombastic?" I was deeply offended, despite the odious circumstances. "Tell me, Colonel Baker, have you ever seen me perform?"

He shook his dark head. "No, but I read the newspapers, Mr. Booth."

"Northern newspapers, no doubt," I said with a snort.

"They aren't exactly known for their equitable treatment of Southern actors."

"Nor are certain Southern editions," he smiled in reply. "But I also know your brother, Junius. We met while I was working with the Vigilance Committee in San Francisco. Even he admits you have a tendency to, as he put it, overact."

I had to look away, seething, and my rancor was further deepened by the sharp, derisive snigger that came from Luther Baker. Stanton only waved his hand vexedly.

"Please continue, colonel."

Col. Baker drew in his breath. "Reputed to be a heavy drinker, fond of gambling, and a notorious womanizer." The last part was added with a raised eyebrow.

It was my turn to smile, broadly. "I'm an actor, gentlemen. Of course I drink. And gamble. And yes, I am not ashamed to admit that the fair sex does seem to find me somewhat attractive. A situation which I find most gratifying." I eyed them both gleefully. "And other men find quite enviable."

Stanton's staid expression never changed, but Baker's thin lips twitched indignantly. The colonel flipped another page.

"Known Southern sympathizer, outspoken in his anti-Union stance, frequently seen in the company of known Copperheads and Confederate loyalists. Smuggler . . ."

I came up out of the chair. "Smuggler? Now wait just a goddamned minute—"

"Sit down, Reb!" Luther Baker's huge paw suddenly grabbed at the back of my collar, while the Colt's cold muzzle pressed in below my ear. The click of the hammer was unnaturally loud in the little room.

Col. Baker and Stanton merely stared at the scene without comment.

The gun shoved in harder. "I said sit down," Luther snarled. "'Less you want me to blow your Secesh head off."

I sat down, slowly, and a nod from Stanton made Luther

back away. "I am not a smuggler," I told them flatly, straightening my coat. "And no one can say that I am."

Col. Baker tapped his pencil against the book. "Do you deny that you arranged for a shipment of medical supplies to be transported from Louisville to Confederate soldiers in Tennessee?"

How in God's Name had they come to know these things? I licked at my lips, which had gone incredibly dry, but feigned my best scowl of disinterest. "I paid for a load of quinine and other medicines to be distributed to Southern wounded. Is it a crime to give aid to wounded men?"

"When those men are the enemy," Col. Baker said.

"Punishable by death," Stanton added quickly. "Tell me, Mr. Booth, with all this fierce Southern loyalty, why is it you never bothered to don the Confederate gray?"

"Why don't you just consult Colonel Baker's miraculous book?" I sighed in disgust. "No doubt he has the answer."

The Secretary's small dark eyes held mine flatly. "Perhaps. But I'm asking you."

"I was something of my mother's favorite as I child," I said with a shrug. "She asked me not to take part in the fighting, and as a dutiful son I obliged. But I was briefly a member of a militia unit. The Richmond Grays," I said proudly. "We assisted in the capture of old John Brown." I turned and grinned smugly at Col. Baker. "Or isn't that in your damnable book?"

"It is," he nodded. "But your unit didn't take part in Brown's capture, Mr. Booth. You merely witnessed his execution."

That was when the bravado, and the strength, finally fled me. "Oh, Christ, that's enough!" I buried my face in my hands. Whatever it was they wanted, it wasn't worth this mindless charade. "You didn't come here to read me the facts of my life. If you have something to say to me, say it! Just don't play this wretched game any longer!"

Stanton glanced at Col. Baker and nodded. "Tell him."

One more time Col. Baker flipped through his book. He cleared his throat, then traced an entry with the tip of a long finger. "On the night of March fifteenth of this year, you attended a private meeting in Gautier's restaurant here in Washington City. With you were six other men; John Harrison Surratt, David E. Herold, Lewis Paine, or Powell," he glanced up at me. "We're not certain of his last name. George Atzerodt, Michael O'Laughlin, and Samuel Arnold. Each of these men are known Confederate sympathizers, and some are suspected spies. In the course of this meeting, the seven of you fashioned a plan to kidnap the President of the United States." Col. Baker looked up from the book, first at Stanton, then at me. "Do you deny this meeting took place, Mr. Booth?"

I drew in my breath, slowly. "No."

"Do you deny that you planned to deliver the president to Richmond and use him as ransom for Confederate prisoners of war?"

"No."

Col. Baker's puzzled gape told me he wasn't prepared for my answer. Even Stanton looked surprised.

"You admit you planned to kidnap Lincoln?" the Secretary demanded.

"Why should I deny it?" I waved a weary hand at Col. Baker, falling back in the chair. "You obviously know more about me than I know about myself. If you'll pardon the pun, sir, my life is an open book."

Stanton turned to Col. Baker with a look of open astonishment. "Well, I must admit, I never thought it would be that simple. Truly, Mr. Booth," he said as he looked back at me, "you are a most unpredictable man. I was certain you would deny everything."

I shook my head bitterly. "To what end, Mr. Stanton? That

is gone, for which I sought to live, and therefore now I need not fear to die. Shakespeare," I said to his curious frown. "And I am not afraid to die, gentlemen. Not in the least."

"Die?" Stanton's scowl suddenly deepened. "What makes you think you're going to die?"

It was my turn to look confused. "Isn't that why you're here? To arrest me for plotting to kidnap our glorious president?"

Ever so slowly, a look of genuine mirth crept across the Secretary's lined face. "Arrest you? Good heavens, no! I have no intentions of arresting you. Absolutely none. Oh, to be certain, if I wanted to, I could haul you and the rest of the men named in that book down to Capitol Prison and hang you straight away from the very gates. But you are far too valuable to be hanged, Mr. Booth. I need you, sir."

"Need me?" I sat up straight, peering from man to blank-faced man in deepening perplexity. "I am a Southerner, a man completely opposed to all you stand for! My whole life has been dedicated to the ruination of the North! How in God's Name could you possibly need me?"

"For those selfsame reasons. You plotted to kidnap the president, which means you're a man of action and resource. Those are qualities I admire. I need both you and your associates, in order to carry out your scheme."

I could only stare at him. "You . . . you want us to kidnap the president?"

"No, Mr. Booth," Stanton said flatly. "I want you to kill him . . . ."

Chapter Five

'Tis strange, and oftentimes, to win us to our harm,
The instruments of darkness tell us truths.
~~~Macbeth~~~

For several incredulous moments, the only sound within the room was the muted roar of revelry beyond the curtained windows. I studied each man's face, in the wavering lamplight, certain my ears had deceived me. But their expressions showed no emotion. no reflection of the gravity of the words that had just been spoken. Col. Baker merely drummed a pair of dispassionate fingers against his notebook. Luther continued to regard me over his Colt like something he had dragged from the sewer. And Stanton himself sat laconically in his chair, with pursed lips and a placid demeanor which suggested he had offered nothing more grievous than an invitation to afternoon tea.

My tongue finally managed to loose itself from its stupefied knot. "This . . . this is some sort of joke, is it not?"

"I never joke, Mr. Booth," the Secretary said earnestly. "You would be well advised to remember that. And please, don't act so surprised. The same thought has often crossed your own mind."

"Never!" I shook my head emphatically. "I never plotted to kill the president! Before God, my intention was solely to use him as ransom for Confederate prisoners!"

"Yes, yes," Stanton growled. "For God and country, etcetera. Please, spare me the patriotic drivel." He reached out and snatched the notebook from Col. Baker's grasp, then swiftly thumbed through the pages. "What a glorious opportunity for immortality awaits the man who would kill Abraham Lincoln." His eyes calmly met mine over the leather bindings. "Your own words, Mr. Booth."

"Damn you!" I fixed the book, and him, with a seething glare. "God damn you straight to hell! How do you know these things? How do you know a man's very soul?"

"Because it's my business to know." He tossed the notebook back to Col. Baker with a neat flip of his hand. "Knowledge is power, Mr. Booth, and power is security. In this case, the security of our great nation." He nodded briefly toward the colonel and Luther. "I have eyes and ears on every street corner, as you yourself have discovered. In every public house, every coach and train; wherever two men can gather for what they believe is private conversation. I can imprison a man with a single word, or end his life with the stroke of a pen. Some have been known simply to disappear." A thin smile cracked his somber mien, just long enough to make the hair on the back of my neck stand on end. "And I can assure you, sir, they will never be heard from again."

I summoned up some little pluck. "And is that to be my fate, Mr. Stanton? Just another nameless victim of Yankee tyranny?"

Stanton spread his small hands. "Such a choice is entirely yours. As I said before, I have no intentions of ending your life. Not as yet. However, I am somewhat puzzled. Why would an actor choose to carry out such a brazen scheme as kidnapping the president?" His sneer was coldly sardonic. "Doesn't your very profession offer enough intrigue?"

I held the mocking glare. "Above all else, Mr. Stanton, I am a patriot. Ever since your murderous General Grant decided to stop paroling Southern prisoners, the Confederate army has been doomed. Lincoln would have been the perfect ransom."

"But why this radical passion for the South to begin with? The rest of your family are such ardent Unionists. Your own brother even saved the life of the president's eldest son."

I recalled the incident to which he referred. Two years

previously, Edwin had been waiting for a train in Jersey City, when the surging crowd had pushed a young bystander between the platform and a moving freight car. Eddie had managed to reach out and pull the man to safety, only to discover that it was Robert Lincoln. As humble a dear soul as my brother was, he rarely spoke of the incident, though privately I knew it was a source of immense pride. I myself would have thrown the bastard back.

"What paths my brothers choose for themselves is their own affair," I told Stanton curtly. "But you can be certain, sir, had it been me on that platform, Mr. Lincoln's whelp would not have been quite so fortunate."

I thought I detected a momentary flash in his dark eyes, as though the Secretary found my reply distinctly amusing. But he quickly shook his gray head. "You still did not answer my question, Mr. Booth. How is it you favor the Confederacy?"

"What's this?" I sat forward suddenly, waving a frantic hand at the colonel's notebook. "Pray tell, sir, do you mean to say that Colonel Baker's sacred tome has lost its power of divination? My God!" I fell back in the chair, rolling my eyes dolefully. "How can the world yet survive?"

My performance was patently lost. "Just answer the question, Mr. Booth."

"To what end, sir? My life is hardly a subject for your draconian archives! But if it is truly that important, I have no cause to embrace your precious Union. The first time I appeared on a northern stage, in Philadelphia, I was booed unmercifully. The critics called me unrefined. They said I was totally bereft of talent! And the same gracious aplomb was afforded me yet again, in New York City. But in Richmond, Mr. Stanton, as in every Southern theater since, I have been embraced with open arms. Believe me," I snarled in contempt, "I know where my loyalties lie."

"Indeed," Stanton nodded, as that same dark smile swiftly

returned. "Which is exactly why I want you to kill the president."

I shook my head in perplexity, rubbing at the merciless pain that had begun to pound between my eyes. "For the love of God, none of this makes any sense! You talk of loyalty to the Union, and preserving its security, but you ask me to kill the very man who fought to save it."

"Because the Union cannot survive unless Lincoln dies," the Secretary said frankly. He stood up, crossing to the same window where I had stood with Prudy, then folded his hands behind his back and stared out at the night's now-fading revelry. "No doubt you find that difficult to understand."

"What I understand," I sighed, "is that one of us has most assuredly gone mad. And I'm reasonably certain it's me."

Stanton laughed at that, a harsh, wheezing snort that ended in a spasm of choked coughing. Col. Baker jumped to his feet, frowning anxiously as he hurried to Stanton's side, but the Secretary brusquely waved him off. He wiped at his mouth with a silk handkerchief and slowly recovered his breath. "I'm all right, colonel, thank you. Just a mild attack." Stanton caught my puzzled look and shrugged thinly. "Asthma. Colonel Baker worries that I shall undoubtedly fall dead at the very next wheeze."

"You've already been found unconscious twice," the colonel grumbled as he returned to his chair.

"Don't worry about me, Colonel Baker," Stanton said grimly. "I have no intentions of departing this life before our beloved Chief Executive." He turned to stare blankly at me. "Tell me, Mr. Booth, what do you think will become of your precious South, now that the war has ended?"

The question caused my gut to roil. "I shudder to even consider the prospects. Ruin and despair under the Union bootheel, no doubt. Especially after Lincoln crowns himself king!"

"King?" Stanton laughed again, but there was precious

little humor in his dark eyes. "Oh, no, the Original Gorilla is far too humble to even consider such a lofty aspiration. He has difficulty in accepting the trappings of the presidency. No, sir, Lincoln will not be king, but neither will he be kind. Southern leaders are to be imprisoned or hanged. Confederate veterans who refuse to swear allegiance to the Union will be denied their Constitutional rights. And do you know his intentions for the Negro?"

I felt my fingernails dig deeper into the chair's upholstery. "I'm not entirely certain I wish to know."

"Equality, sir. Equality with the white man, at least in the North." Stanton's eyes were waiting for my sudden, horrified glance. "Yes, indeed, Mr. Booth. Domination in the South. Those who wielded the taskmaster's whip will now be forced to feel it. Congressmen, magistrates, lawmen; wherever a position of authority exists, a black man will hold it. Think of it, sir. Imagine the horror, if you can. White men subjected to Negro law. White women thrown to the mercy of black lust. Can you see it, Mr. Booth?" The Secretary walked closer to me, dark eyes burning with a livid, festering rage. "Can you see that wretched evil? My God, the very angels in Heaven will cry out with anguish!" He leaned over my chair, pressing close enough that I could feel the heat of his wheezing breath and the flecks of angry spittle. "Can you live with that evil, Mr. Booth?"

"Jesus God," I whispered hoarsely. "Can't you stop him? Can't you use your own influence to change his mind?"

"Influence?" Stanton stood straight up, blinking rapidly behind his spectacles. "He is the president, sir. He is beloved by the people. He has won his war and is lauded like Caesar in triumph! No one can influence him now." The Secretary turned away and stood for several pensive moments near the bed. I watched as he reached out and picked up Prudy's tiny pistol, turning it over and over within his diminutive hands.

"No one can influence him now."

He whirled around to suddenly face me. "That is why I need your help, Mr. Booth."

I stared at him, still uncertain as to the very reality of this impossible nightmare. "Mr. Stanton, you are a member of the president's own cabinet! How can you even speak this way? How is it you can hold such a convivial attitude toward the South, when you tried so hard to destroy her? How can you, Lincoln's own—"

"Friend?" Stanton finished angrily. "Lincoln's own friend? Is that what you were going to say, Mr. Booth? Well, let me tell you, sir, I am not Lincoln's friend. I have never been that . . . that baboon's friend! Four years," he hissed through clenched teeth. "Four interminable years! That's how long I've had to watch as he's made a mockery of the very office he holds! I have seen him laugh, at his own backwoods buffoonery, when thousands of good men were dying! I have listened to his inane jests, suffered through his melancholy moods, and even put up with his addled wife and his incorrigible brats! But I am damned if I will stand idle and watch as this country is destroyed by his demented sense of charity toward the goddamned niggers!"

He looked down at me ruefully. "I am no friend of the South, Mr. Booth, but neither am I her worst enemy. Do as I ask, and you may very well save both her and yourself." Slowly, he raised the pistol towards my face. "Refuse, and you will both die a most ignominious death."

For the second time that night, I found myself staring into the single unblinking eye of that damnable derringer. I looked away, locking instead on Stanton's withering glare. "If I agree to kill Lincoln," I ventured warily, "what will I receive in return?"

He lowered the gun. "Your country's unspoken gratitude, for one thing."

Despite my frenzied trembling, I could not help a bitter laugh. "My country? Christ, that's rich! I have no country. You bastards have seen to that. No, sir, I prefer something decidedly more tangible."

"You are hardly in a position to demand anything, Mr. Booth. But what exactly do you want?"

"Freedom, of course, once the deed is done. An unhindered escape route, time to flee, and enough money to get me as far away from Washington City as is humanly possible."

Stanton frowned sharply. "And how much would that be?"

I leaned back in my chair, feeling slightly less apprehensive now. "Five hundred thousand dollars."

Luther Baker let out an incredulous whistle behind me, while the colonel's impassive face suddenly went ghostly white. Stanton only pulled his irascible scowl deeper.

"That's an exorbitant sum. For a man facing his own demise, you ask a great deal."

I loosed a mocking snort. "And you do not? In any event, you won't kill me, Mr. Stanton. As you said yourself, you need me."

He shook his head, amused enough to smile again. "Really, Mr. Booth, don't overestimate your own worth. The amount may not be to your liking."

"My performances are never cheap," I shrugged. "Just ask any theater manager. And they may very well be . . . bombastic, as Colonel Baker claims, but I can assure you they are no less histrionic than yours."

There was a sudden, startled flicker in his eyes. "What do you mean by that?"

"Exactly what I said. For all of your so-called power, Mr. Stanton, you are a very transparent man. You didn't come here to intimidate me. You came because you know I'm the only man in all of Washington capable of doing what you ask. After all, I could have easily killed Lincoln last month, during his inauguration, had it truly been my intention. I stood on a balcony less than ten feet above his head, thanks to a ticket provided me by Senator Hale's daughter." I threw a wry smile towards Colonel Baker's insufferable notebook. "Although I'm certain you already know that. Just as you also know that I have free and absolute reign of this entire city. There isn't a door in the capital that isn't open to Wilkes Booth." I folded my arms across my chest, enjoying his frustrated glare. It was a bold gambit, to be certain, but I had nothing left to lose. "If anyone can get close enough to kill your president, sir, I can. And I believe that's worth a tidy sum."

Stanton studied me silently over the rim of his spectacles, and for a single terrifying moment, when I caught the flare of the hissing lamp in his narrowed eyes, I thought that I might have pushed my luck just the slightest bit too far. Then, slowly, he nodded. "Very well. Five hundred thousand dollars, payable on completion of the event."

"Payable now," I said flatly. "Or there will be no 'event'."

Stanton's eyes flew wide, and even Col. Baker jumped up from the table.

"Not in cash," I said quickly, holding up my hand. "And not here. Not in Washington. I want the money deposited in the Ontario Bank of Montreal, where I already have an account for my oil leases under the name J. Wilkes. There's a man in Canada, Jacob Thompson, who serves as the Canadian controller of Confederate funds. He doesn't care much for Yankees, but he'll handle their money right enough. Once I receive a telegram from Thompson advising me that the funds are in my account, then I'll kill your Mr. Lincoln."

Colonel Baker glanced pleadingly at Stanton. "This is goddamned outrageous! Let me kill the bastard right now!" I heard his cousin step in closer behind me, as the colonel groped for his pistol.

"No," Stanton sighed, waving them both off. "Let him be."

He turned back to me. "Half, Mr. Booth. I'll deposit half the money in your account, and the remainder once Lincoln is dead. And that, sir, is my final offer."

I nodded once, satisfied. "Agreed. Now then, how do you want me to do it?"

"I don't give the slightest damn. You have your own resources. Shoot him, club him, or cut his miserable throat, for that matter."

"When?"

Stanton didn't answer. Instead, he picked up Col. Baker's notebook one more time. "Your kidnapping attempt was to take place in Ford's Theater, was it not?"

It still troubled me as to how he knew these facts so intimately. Had Luther or another of Stanton's minions somehow been present during our meetings? Or, which was a far more likely conjecture, had one of my own companions turned Judas? The very thought sent waves of horror coursing through my soul.

"It was," I nodded warily.

The Secretary looked up at me. "Did you know that Lincoln once saw you perform there? He was rather impressed, in fact. Said he applauded you quite fervently."

"Really? I would have preferred the applause of a nigger."

Stanton flashed his thin little smile. "The Lincolns will be attending a theatrical performance this coming Friday. I don't know which one, but I'm certain they'll go. Mrs. Lincoln has made the theater another of her lunatic obsessions. And if she doesn't persuade the president to accompany her, then I will. I would surmise your best opportunity would be to strike at some point during the play."

"But which theater?" I demanded. "Ford's or Grover's?"

"I don't know," he shrugged curtly. "I'll contact you when I find out. What I do know is that you can be absolutely certain Mr. Lincoln will arrive with few or no bodyguards."

"What about my escape? The roads out of the city are guarded day and night. I had the devil's own time getting back in from Boston. I don't want to run into a Federal patrol ten minutes after I've killed the bastard."

Stanton placed the book aside. "I swear to you, Mr. Booth, there will be no interference, by anyone, before, during, or after you make your move. Let me know your escape route, and I'll provide you with a password to facilitate your exit from Washington."

I scowled at him sardonically. "With all due respect, Mr. Secretary, just how am I supposed to contact you? Leave a message at the War Department?"

He shook his head briefly. "No, at the Kirkwood Hotel. For Vice-President Johnson."

I gaped at him. "Johnson?"

"He knows nothing," Stanton quickly affirmed. "He's a drunken fool who spends the bulk of his day sleeping off the night before. The perfect replacement for the Illinois Ape, in fact. Just leave a note for him at the front desk. I'll have it intercepted."

The Secretary tugged a watch from his vest pocket, frowned over the time, then reached out for his hat which was draped over a bedpost. "If you will excuse us, Mr. Booth, I see the hour is quite late. We shall take our leave of you now." He nodded to the Bakers, who swiftly proceeded him to the door. "One more thing," he said suddenly, stopping to scowl back at me. "It is in your best interest to tell no one, not even your confederates, of this meeting. And whatever you do, don't fix it within your mind to leave Washington City. Remember," he said, flicking a sidelong glance towards Luther Baker. "My eyes and ears are everywhere."

I had to shake my head in grudging admiration. "You have everything in hand, haven't you? All written out, just like a play. What a pity you never tried your hand at the theater, Mr.

Stanton. Who knows, you might even have been as celebrated as myself."

The sudden sneer that flashed across his bearded face was as deathly cold as it was contemptuous. "Oh, but I already am, Mr. Booth," he said as he tugged on his hat. "Even so, it was still a tremendous pleasure to meet such a distinguished luminary as yourself. Good evening to you, sir."

Luther Baker tugged open the door, and the three of them were swiftly, mercifully gone.

I sat there, devoid of feeling, for God alone knows how long, staring blankly at the oak-paneled door and scarcely able to draw a breath. I managed to catch my reflection, in the little mirror above the washstand, and the face that leered incredulously back at me was as stark and pale as a corpse. I, John Wilkes Booth, prince of players, had just conspired to embark upon the greatest performance of my life. But the stage for this production, as I realized with a sudden trembling rush, was history itself, and the tyrant slain would be no mere thespian scoundrel. I was going to kill Abraham Lincoln.

The President of the United States.

Chapter Six

Between the acting of a dreadful thing
And the first motion, all the interim is
Like a phantasma or a hideous dream.
      ~~~Julius Caesar~~~

The knocking jolted me awake.

I glanced around, blinking at the dusty sunlight that filtered through the curtains, and for a single blessed moment, I was certain the entire occurrence had been a dream. An alcoholic chimera, I yawned in relief, soon to be ruefully slain by a copious hair of the dog. But then I looked down, and I realized that I was still slumped in the armchair, fully clothed, and my rising elation vanished in a groan of despair.

The knocking sounded again, loud enough to finally penetrate the fog within my brain. Someone was banging at my door.

I bolted from the chair, fairly leaping across the room to snatch up Prudy's gun and the dagger, then slowly approached the door. Stanton's cronies, bastards that they were, would hardly have bothered to knock. Yet I took no chances, cocking the gun and sliding the knife through my belt before I closed a violently trembling hand around the brass knob.

"Who . . . who is it?

"Mr. Booth?" A muffled voice, youthful and familiar, called out anxiously. "Mr. Booth, are you in there, sir? It's me, sir. Davey."

"Christ Almighty!" I nearly swooned against the door, so great was my relief. I shoved the derringer into a pocket and yanked open the door. "Davey!"

The face that smiled broadly up at mine was thin, boyish, and welcome beyond words. Davey Herold was twenty-two, a short, dark-headed youth with small dark eyes and a perpetual grin, as though the world itself were his private jest. I had met him outside of Ford's theater one cold night some two years before, when a group of Maryland sympathizers had come to offer praise for both my performance and my Confederate stand. The youngest child, and the only male, in a family of eight children, Davey worked as an apothecary's assistant in Thompson's Drug Store to help support his widowed mother. He told me how he had once mixed a heavy dose of purgatives into a tonic that had been prescribed for President Lincoln himself. The thought of Old Abe, trotting through the White House for the sinks, had given me a grand laugh, and the boy and I quickly became friends. Davey was a simple youth, though some coldly called him stupid, yet he was steadfast, deeply religious, and, when it came to the Cause, had not the slightest dearth of allegiance.

Davey's irrepressible grin suddenly faded, as his twinkling eyes rapidly took in my disheveled appearance. "Jesus, Mr. Booth! Are you all right, sir? You look like death itself!"

"Death would be a welcome respite, Davey boy," I sighed wearily. "Why don't you—" I glanced past him, then suddenly stiffened in alarm, thrusting my hand into my pocket when I saw that he was not alone.

"You know Mr. Wiechmann, don't you, sir?" Davey jerked a thumb at the tall, broad-shouldered young man that hovered behind him. "He rooms over at Mrs. Surratt's." Davey shook his head at my wary scowl. "He's a friend of John's, Mr. Booth. Remember?"

It took me a moment, but I finally placed the blue-eyed, fair-skinned face that stared impassively back at me. A divinity student, as I recalled, though his stocky frame was more in keeping with a prizefighter than a preacher. "Yes, of course," I nodded, still fingering the pistol. "Louis, isn't it?"

He bobbed his blond head. "Yes, sir, Louis. How are you,

Mr. Booth?"

"I've been better." I glanced furtively past both of them, down either side of the red-carpeted corridor, then looked at Davey. "What brings the two of you here?"

"Mrs. Surratt wants to know if she can borrow your horse an' buggy, Mr. Booth. She wants Louis an' me to drive her down to Lloyd's Tavern so she can collect a debt. I told her you'd likely lend it to her, sir." He frowned at me, warily, like a penitent child. "Was I wrong, sir?"

"Of course not, Davey. And I'd be happy to help, except I returned the rig yesterday, just after I returned from Boston. But I'll gladly rent her another." I started to dig through my clothes, then remembered with an angry start that the Bakers had relieved me of my effects. I glanced around the room, sighing in relief when I saw the money, as well as my watch and stickpin, piled in a heap on the tangled bedclothes. A true miracle, I mused as I retrieved the items. Yankees who hadn't been thieves.

"Here," I peeled off a twenty-dollar note as I returned to the door. "Take this over to Howard's stable and tell him to give you the best he has." I handed the money to Wiechmann.

Davey grinned again, lifting two fingers to his dark curls. "Thank you, Mr. Booth, sir. I knew you'd help. We'll be goin' now."

"Wait a moment, Davey." I looked up at Wiechmann. "Would you mind taking care of the widow by yourself, Louis? I have business with Davey here, if he's available."

The blond youth shrugged indifferently. "Yes, sir, I don't see why not." He glanced down, frowning curiously, and I followed his leery gaze to the dagger tucked in my belt. Wiechmann looked back up at me, still scowling, but merely waved the banknote. "I'll bring you back what's left over, Mr. Booth."

"Keep it," I shrugged. "And give the widow my best

regards."

Wiechmann's blue eyes widened appreciatively, but never lost their guarded cast. "Thank you, sir. I'll do just that." He nodded his leave and trudged off, tossing a final suspicious frown in my direction.

I watched until his lumbering bulk had disappeared down the stairs, and a sudden baleful quiver swept over me. Was it possible Louis was responsible for Stanton's insufferable knowledge? Despite the youth's close friendship with the widow's son, John, who was an intimate player in my clandestine company, I was reasonably certain Wiechmann had never been privy to our plans. Or had he?

I shrugged off the chill, like a winter's cloak, but couldn't easily dismiss my trepidation. No one could be trusted now. Absolutely no one.

Except, of course, for Davey.

"Come on inside, Davey," I said with a grateful smile. "You have no idea how much I could use a friendly face."

Davey cocked his dark head anxiously, as I swiftly closed the door behind him. "Are you all right, Mr. Booth? I ain't never seen you like this." His eyes lost their carefree gleam. "There ain't no trouble, is there?"

"Trouble?" I clapped a hand on his thin shoulder. "You have a remarkable talent for understatement, Davey boy. As Hamlet said, time is out of joint." I lowered my voice, despite the fact that we were alone. *Wherever two men can gather for what they believe is private conversation . . . .* "Tell me, how many of the others are here in Washington?"

He thought for a moment. "I ain't real sure, Mr. Booth. I know John's home, 'cause Louis an' I just come from the widow's. Mr. Paine is around someplace, I reckon, an' so's George. I don't know about Sam and Mr. O'Laughlin."

I nodded, pressing a wad of bills into his hand. "Do me a favor, then. Run downstairs and fetch me a bottle of brandy, then go and see if you can find the others. Have everyone meet me at the widow's at noon."

"But it's nearly noon now, Mr. Booth."

"That late? Christ Almighty!" I pulled out my watch and scowled over the time. Davey was right, it was already eleven-fifteen. "Well then, make it one o'clock. And be quick about it. I need to get everyone together as soon as possible. We still have business to complete."

"Business?" Davey shoved the money into a trouser pocket, eyeing me in bewilderment. "I don't understand, Mr. Booth. The war's over, ain't it?"

"Nothing's over, Davey boy. Our plans have merely changed, that's all." I slapped his shoulder again. "Hurry back with that brandy, will you? I haven't had breakfast yet."

He was gone and back within a few minutes, with a bottle of the hotel's best stock, bless his soul. Then he was off again, whistling through that immutable smile, and I hurriedly began my morning's ablutions.

The brandy did an excellent job of calming my nerves, especially as I was in sore need of a shave, and I didn't trust the razor in my shaking hands. But half a bottle later I was neatly groomed, and actually starting to feel like myself again. I changed into a new suit of clothes, concealed the weapons beneath my coat, then snatched up what was left of the brandy and left the room.

The clerk behind the desk smiled cheerily as I descended the lobby staircase. "Good morning, Mr. Booth!"

"Go to hell," I snarled, hurrying past his startled gape with scarcely a glance.

Despite the hour, there were only a handful of diners in the hotel's public room. Most of them showed the effects of last night's festivities, though I was grimly certain none could have boasted of my own adventures. The cavernous room, with its sea of white-linen circlets, was deathly quiet, save for the muted tinkle of silver and china, and I was grateful for the fact that no one seemed in a talkative mood. I ordered a meal from a bleary-eyed waiter and ate in solitude, then procured another bottle of their impeccable brandy and waited, lost in my dismal thoughts, until it was time to leave for Widow Surratt's.

It was five minutes until one when I crossed the busy intersection at 6th and H Streets. The traffic was busier than normal this bright spring day, though my attention was hardly focused on the wagonloads of refugees and homeward-trudging soldiers. The devil's bargain I had made with Stanton seemed to grow more and more perplexing with every hurried step. What in God's Name had I stumbled into? I was dedicated to the Cause; no man could argue that. I would gladly die before I would watch the South ground into the dust by Union vengeance. And in perfect truth, the thought of killing the Original Gorilla was no more iniquitous to me than squashing a cockroach. But to kill Lincoln at the behest of the very men he trusted most? Good Christ, had the world truly gone that insane?

I nearly passed the Surratt house, in my anxious haste, and trotted swiftly up the outside stairs to the second-story entrance. I tapped at the whitewashed door with my cane, glancing around to make certain I hadn't been followed. Yet I knew it was a futile hope, for somewhere, in a nearby doorway or shadowed alley, Luther Baker or another of Stanton's diabolical minions was most assuredly lurking. The very thought made my flesh crawl.

The door swung open, and an incredibly pretty face suddenly made the day seem far less vexing.

"Mr. Booth! Davey said you were coming! Come in, sir, please!"

I tipped my hat, with a final furtive glance over my shoulder. "Good afternoon, Anna. You're looking as lovely as ever. Might I be invited in?"

"Of course," she laughed, stepping away from the door. "Mother would never forgive me if I allowed the great John Wilkes Booth to languish on our doorstep!"

"Hardly great," I smiled as I hurried inside. "Celebrated at the most, harried at the very least." I bent to gently kiss her hand. "And always at the service of beautiful ladies."

Anna Surratt was indeed a beautiful young woman. She had dark eyes and long raven hair, pulled back in the current fashion, and the coiled ringlets framed delicate features and full red lips. Her dress was dark muslin, with a gay froth of lace about her porcelain neck, but the material did little to conceal enticingly nubile curves. Yet as alluring as the twenty-two year-old was, I would never have attempted to divest her of that clothing. I had far too much respect for Anna and her entire family.

The Surratts were devout Catholics, a religion shared by my own mother, and Anna's widowed mother, Mary Surratt, treated me as though I were one of her own offspring. The widow was also a staunch Rebel, and within her humble walls I found a solace and a hospitality unlike any I had ever known. The very thought that I could deliberately bring shame upon this house, or to any of the widow's family, was coldly anathema.

Anna laughed again, drawing her hand back demurely, but it was plain to see the crimson hue that rose in her lovely cheeks. She quickly relieved me of my hat and walking stick. "Will you be staying long, Mr. Booth? Mother had to travel to Lloyd's this morning, but she should be back soon."

"I know. I saw Mr. Wiechmann when he came to secure a tack. Perhaps I'll see her before I leave."

I glanced around the tiny foyer. The house was clean, but extremely spartan, and badly in need of repairs. Despite numerous boarders, all of whom dutifully paid their rent, the widow still had difficulty in meeting her financial obligations. Her husband had died a disreputable drunk, with far more debts than debtors, and the family had been forced to leave a larger, far more lucrative establishment in the village of Surrattsville, just across the Potomac in Maryland. The widow had leased the inn to a man named Lloyd, then moved her two children to this rambling ten-room affair in Washington City. I had offered to assist the dear lady in meeting her debts, with funds of my own, but a single piercing glare from her dark eyes had ended the matter, permanently.

"You said Davey told you I was coming," I said as I turned back to Anna. "Is he here?"

She nodded, pointing to a nearby set of sliding doors. "In the parlor. John is with him, and so is Mr. Paine." She made a sudden, abhorrent face. "And so is that horrid little man from the sticks."

I had to laugh. "You mean George?"

Anna held her rancid grimace. "Whatever his name is, he's absolutely disgusting. I don't understand how you can associate with trash like that, Mr. Booth!"

"Desperate times, my dear Anna, call for desperate allies. Don't worry about George, he's harmless." I started towards the parlor door.

Anna stepped forward eagerly. "Should I fetch you some coffee, Mr. Booth?"

"No!" I snapped, much too quickly. "I mean, no thank you, Anna. I wish to speak to the others in private." I kissed her hand again, meeting her jeweled eyes with my most charming grin. "You do understand, of course?"

She blushed once more. "Why, of course. Well, if you'll excuse me, I have a lot of work to do."

Anna disappeared down a nearby hallway, and I turned once again to the parlor. I took a deep breath, slid the door open, and stepped inside.

"Gentlemen," I smiled to the waiting group. "It's good to see you all again. I have the most tremendous news . . ."

Chapter Seven

Treason and murder ever kept together,
As two yoke-devils sworn to either's purpose.
~~~Henry V~~~

Davey Herold sat on a small velvet settee, twisting his hat between nervous hands, and flashed me his familiar grin.

John Surratt, the widow's son, stood near the fireplace, puffing intently on a soldier's clay pipe as he nodded his hello. John was a year younger than his sister, but in appearance he seemed a great deal older. This was partly due to a thick mustache, which he'd grown to divert attention from an exceedingly narrow chin. But his true maturity came from his avocation. John was a spy, a Confederate courier, and had been since the tender age of seventeen. He knew the back roads and backwater trails from Richmond to Baltimore like the back of his thin hands, and had even carried vital messages to loyalist sympathizers as far north as Canada. I truly admired the boy, as he had risked capture and certain death almost daily for the past four interminable years. He was well-educated, even having once studied for the priesthood, and was easily the most intelligent of all my comrades. I looked upon him as a trusted right hand, and, like Davey, I knew it was absolutely impossible for John to have been our Judas.

Yet I was not at all so certain when it came to the others.

George Atzerodt, the 'horrid little man from the sticks', as Anna called him, grinned his stupid, broken-toothed leer from his sprawl in a floral armchair. George was in his thirties—the oldest of our band—a squat, ugly little German immigrant who spoke broken English and had both the appearance and the mentality of a back-alley drunk. He wore a gray suit that I myself had paid for, part of an ungodly sum

I had already lavished on our plan, but what had once been fashionable enough for an inaugural ball was now a reeking canvas of mud and beer stains. Atzerodt was hardly my most favorable choice for an ally, yet he had his particular usefulness. He was a blacksmith from Port Tobacco, a worthless sinkhole in the Maryland swamps, and he had worked as a smuggler and blockade runner to augment his meager income. George knew the Maryland peninsula nearly as well as John, and he owned a small boat, which had made him a key performer in our plot to abduct the president. George was to have ferried us all across the Potomac, once we had nabbed Old Abe. Now he would serve the same purpose, after we had killed the bastard. I met George's bloodshot eyes and tried to return his drunken smirk without gagging.

The last man in the little room, standing well apart from the others, was at the same time the biggest, the quietest, and, without question, the most dangerous. Lewis Paine leaned against a corner wall, swathed like a Pharaoh's mummy in a filthy gray overcoat, and regarded me with a look of bemused serenity. And yet, as I paused to peer deeper into his dark blue eyes, I could see something else just beneath the cerulean surface. Something cold, and dark, and completely unnerving.

At only twenty years of age, Paine was already a bull of a man, well over six feet in height, with coal black hair, handsome features, and an oddly halcyon personality. He claimed to have served as a guerrilla raider with the Gray Ghost, John Mosby, and, as Col. Baker himself had mentioned, sometimes used the surname Powell. There was nothing unusual in this, since Confederate soldiers who had been captured and paroled, as Lewis also boasted, often used aliases to reenlist. But along with his myriad identities came rumors of a murderous past, which, when added to the shroud behind those tranquil eyes, only bolstered my apprehension. Lewis was to have spirited Lincoln bodily out of the theater, had our plan succeeded, and I had no real cause to suspect his loyalty. Like Davey, Lewis was as devoted as a hound. But where Davey was my trusted lapdog, Lewis was a mastiff. And far more likely to turn on his master.

Lewis inclined his huge dark head, with a curling sneer that substituted for a smile. "Cap'n," he drawled, his favorite moniker for nearly everyone. "Welcome back."

"Lewis," I nodded in return. "John, Davey, George. Where are Michael and Sam?"

"I can't find Sam nowheres, Mr. Booth," Davey said with a remorseful shrug. "An' Mr. O'Laughlin said he didn't feel like comin'. Said he was through with all this business."

"Did he?" This was extremely interesting. "Did he, indeed?" Sam Arnold and Michael O'Laughlin had always been fringe members of our band, willing flesh but weak spirits, despite the fact that Arnold had been a childhood companion to my brothers and me. Both of them had served as Confederate soldiers, and had always seemed to be trustworthy. But perhaps one or the other had fallen under Stanton's ruthless scrutiny. Perhaps they had been coerced, or even threatened, and revealed their knowledge out of fear.

Or perhaps, just like me, they had merely been bought.

"Jesus . . ." I whispered bitterly.

"Sir?"

"Nothing, Davey, nothing. It doesn't matter, in any event. The five of us are more than sufficient."

"Sufficient for what, Wilkes?" John Surratt tapped his pipe against the fireplace bricks, then brushed a stray ash from his natty suit. "What news are you talking about? Davey mentioned something about a change of plans?" He cocked a wary eyebrow. "The war's over. We can't go on with the plot."

I offered a pithy shrug. "If you are referring to the plan to abduct the Original Gorilla, then you are correct. But who said the war was over? No, gentlemen, the war is ended when the last shot has been fired. And it will be our responsibility to fire it."

Davey frowned curiously from John to me. "Fire it at who, Mr. Booth?"

"At President Lincoln, Davey boy."

There was a sudden, collective gasp of disbelief.

"*Gott in Himmel*." I heard Atzerodt croak. "Shoot Mr. Lincoln?"

I nodded silently, flicking a pensive glance from face to incredulous face. Davey sat with his mouth agape, while Paine hardly moved a muscle. I thought I even detected a brief, almost humorous glimmer in Lewis' cold stare. John only shook his head, as his dark eyes widened balefully.

"Jesus, Wilkes! You can't be serious!"

"I've never been more serious in my entire life."

"But he's the president," John rasped. "The President of the United States!"

"Jefferson Davis is the only president I acknowledge," I said tersely. "And I thought he was yours, as well."

"He is," John sputtered. "Or rather, he was. Dear God, Wilkes, what kind of madness is this?"

"Madness?" I gaped at him, sincerely confused. "For God's sake, John, I'm talking about the salvation of the entire South! Don't you understand? With Lincoln dead, the Confederacy is avenged!"

"*Mein Gott*, Mr. Booth!" Atzerodt shook his greasy head emphatically. "We kill the president, they hang us! They hang us all, *ja*?"

I sighed in disgust. "For your information, my dear Prussian oaf, that noose was slipped about our necks the first time we ever assembled. And if you'll pardon the pun, better to hang for a sheep than a lamb. Besides . . ." I stared exultantly at each of them. "What if I could promise that no one would interfere with our plan, either before or after

Lincoln was killed. What if I could guarantee there would be no bodyguards, no soldiers, no one of any consequence standing between us and the president? Would you agree to it then?"

John loosed an incredulous snort. "And just how do you propose to accomplish that little miracle? What do you plan to do, pay the entire Union Army to look the other way? I know you have money, Wilkes, but no one is that rich!"

"It won't cost me a single dime," I said with a glib smile. "In fact, I intend to make a profit on the deal."

"A profit? From whom?" John's slender face darkened in perplexity. "What's going on here, Wilkes? Just what the hell is all of this about?"

I shook my head slowly. "I can't tell you that, John. Suffice it to say that ours is not the only desire to see Mr. Lincoln laid low. There are those whose interests are, shall we say, reciprocal?"

"Reciprocal? You mean they'll pay us for killing the president? Jesus Christ, that's treason!"

I fixed him with a baffled, yet seethingly scornful glare. "Treason? Since when did you become a goddamn Yankee? I seem to recall that you were a quite willing participant when we planned to waylay the son of a bitch! Why is killing him suddenly so abhorrent?"

"That was different!" John shook the pipe stem at me, a grimace of genuine anguish twisting his face. "That was for a purpose, Wilkes. We had a chance then. There was still hope for the Cause." His rank scowl deepened. "This . . . this is just for revenge! Posterity will call us murderers!"

"Union posterity," I growled through clenched teeth. "Southern patriots will remember us with honor!" I glared at each of them, my breath rising as rapidly as my fury. "Listen to me, all of you. I have always known that I was a man of destiny. It is my intention to carve a niche next to Caesar and

Napoleon themselves, and perhaps even higher! I can do this alone, and I will, if necessary. But I'd like to think there's at least one man among you brave enough to take his place in history! Am I right?"

They glanced back and forth, furtively, each face an anxious mask of the other's. Davey wrung his hat once again, while Atzerodt rubbed a filthy hand across his stubbled jaw. John leaned against the fireplace, shaking his head mournfully, and I heard the pipe suddenly snap within his white-knuckled fist. Paine merely held his languid stoicism.

"Count me in, Cap'n," Lewis suddenly rumbled. "I'll help you kill the bastard."

I nodded. "Thank you, Lewis. What about you, George?"

The German peered at me through splayed fingers. "I don't know, Mr. Booth. All them soldiers, they don't let Lincoln alone!"

"I told you, George, there won't be any soldiers. No police, no bodyguards, no one. Besides, you won't have to be part of the killing. All you have to do is wait for us in Port Tobacco with your boat, just like before." I fought back a contemptuous scowl. "Think you could handle that?"

He frowned up at me. "I just wait with boat, *ja*?"

"*Ja*," I parroted. "You just wait with boat."

He thought for a moment, then finally nodded. "*Ja*!" he said with his idiot grin. "*Ja*, I am with you, Mr. Booth!"

I looked at Davey. "What about you, Davey boy? Can I count on my old friend?"

The boy shrugged. "Hell, I reckon I ain't never made no secret of how I feel about Mr. Lincoln." He offered me a sudden, almost worshipful smile. "Or about you, Mr. Booth. I reckon I'm in, too."

I returned the smile, then turned to John Surratt. "Well, John, that only leaves you. How about it? Do you throw your lot in with the rest of us, or are you the coward I never took you to be?"

He bristled at that, throwing the broken halves of his pipe into the empty fireplace. "I'm not a coward," he snapped, but he held my angry glare with a hesitant frown. His tongue flicked across trembling lips. "How . . . how do you intend to do it?"

"Same as the kidnapping plan," I shrugged. We wait till Lincoln's in the theater. Lewis will cover my back, you and Davey will wait outside with the horses, and I'll shoot the bastard while he watches the play." I finished with a triumphant grin. "Then we'll ride like hell out of Washington and split enough money to live like kings."

John glanced away, still frowning. "When?"

"Friday night."

"This Friday?" John turned back to me, and a look of sheer horror flickered through his dark eyes. "That's Good Friday, Wilkes!"

I shrugged again. "So?"

"So? I'm not so certain the Almighty would condone a murder committed on Good Friday! Can't you choose another day?"

"No. I can't. And besides, from what I know of the Almighty, I can't see as how He condones a murder committed on any day. But this isn't a murder, John, this is retribution. A tyrant facing his due. If anything, God Himself will sanctify our actions."

John's face went deathly pale. "Jesus, Wilkes! Don't blaspheme!"

"Maybe we should all pray," Davey said suddenly.

I saw Paine roll his dark eyes. "Oh, shit."

"Davey's right," I said sharply. "It wouldn't hurt to invoke a blessing or two. We may need it." I nodded at the boy. "Go ahead, Davey."

Davey bowed his dark head and pressed tightly curled fists

against his forehead. For several silent moments, I watched his thin lips work anxiously, earnestly, as he made his appeal to a God, who, as far as I was concerned, cherished the South as deeply as ourselves. Finally, the boy lifted his head with a beatific smile. "Amen!"

"Amen," I echoed sincerely, along with George and John. Paine merely shook his head in disgust.

I slipped a hand on Davey's shoulder. "Thank you, Davey. I truly appreciate that." I looked up at John once again. "Well, John? You never gave me an answer."

He spread his hands. "Wilkes, look, I don't—"

There was a sudden rapid tap at the parlor door.

The five of us whirled as one, as George and Davey leapt quickly to their feet. Paine's huge bulk moved far faster than I thought possible, and he was at the door in the blink of an anxious eye. A LeMat revolver materialized almost magically in his giant fist.

I waved Lewis away, shushing the others to silence, then slowly cracked the door and peered through. "Yes? Who is it?"

"Only me, Mr. Booth."

I caught a glimpse of gingham and lace, and instantly recognized the soft feminine tones. Sighing in relief, I motioned to Lewis to secrete his gun, then opened the door.

"Mrs. Surratt! What a tremendous delight to see you again!"

"Mr. Booth," the widow smiled. "I'm so glad you've returned to Washington. It's always such a pleasure to have you here." She lifted a silver tray, which I saw was laden with chipped china and a platter of warm gingerbread. "Anna said you were meeting with John and the others, and I thought you might enjoy some coffee and cake."

I bowed graciously, waving her inside. "How could we possibly refuse, dear lady? Yet no confection could ever compare to the cherished sweetness of yourself."

"Really, Mr. Booth!" She laughed coyly as she entered, with the same rosy blush that Anna had displayed. Yet I caught a look of almost girlish glee in her eyes as she set the tray on a small table.

Mary Surratt was in her mid-forties, but still quite attractive, despite the tiny lines of age and toil that had invariably begun to track across her slender face. She wore her black hair tied back severely, and always tended to wear dark and unassuming attire, as she was now, which was part of her humble and deeply pious nature. The only real adornment she permitted herself was a pair of gold earrings, which, according to John, had been a gift from her late husband. Memories of a much sweeter time, I could only wistfully assume. She was a truly wonderful woman, as dear to me as my own mother, and I cherished her quite dearly.

The widow smiled at each of us, even the reeking George, and waved work-worn hands toward the platter. "Please, gentlemen, help yourselves. And I don't want to find so much as a crumb remaining when I come to collect those dishes!"

I laughed. "If you made it, dear lady, then you can rest assured it will be devoured with gluttonous abandon."

"*Ja*," Atzerodt grinned. "Don't you worry none, missus! I eat what they don't!" The grimy pig stuffed an entire slab of gingerbread into his whiskered maw.

Mrs. Surratt tactfully glanced away. "Yes, well, Mr. Booth, I wanted to thank you for providing Mr. Wiechmann and myself with the rig this morning."

"Think nothing of it. It was my distinct pleasure."

She reached into a pocket of her soiled apron. "Nonetheless, Louis told me that you gave him twenty dollars for the rental. Here is your change." She held out a small wad of bills. "I intend to pay you back the remainder, of course, once I can afford it. I only hope you will be kind enough to wait a short while?"

I waved the proffered money aside. "Please, Mrs. Surratt, I told Louis to keep what was left. There's no need to repay me."

She fixed me with those flashing dark eyes, pressing the money firmly into my hand. "Please, Mr. Booth, I insist. I cannot abide charity, however gracious it may be. Surely you can understand?"

I took the banknotes reluctantly. "As you wish, dear lady. But if you ever need anything."

She nodded quickly, glancing away with an obvious flush of embarrassment. "Yes, yes, of course. You're far too kind." She turned to frown curiously at John, who still held his pasty-faced glower. "Well, John, aren't you at least going to say hello to your mother?"

"You'll have to forgive John, dear lady," I said swiftly. "He isn't quite himself today. Are you, John?"

He glanced away without a reply.

Mrs. Surratt shook her head in maternal chagrin, then smiled at the rest of us. "Well, if you'll excuse me, gentlemen, I'll leave you to finish your business." She started out of the parlor, then turned to offer me a wan look. "I suppose it's a blessing that the war is finally over, is it not, Mr. Booth?"

"A mixed blessing," I said bleakly.

"God moves in mysterious ways," the widow mused. "Perhaps He'll have an answer for us all, someday."

I glanced briefly at the others. "Maybe even sooner than we might expect."

"Perhaps," she said quietly. "Good afternoon, Mr. Booth."

I bowed once more. "Good afternoon, dear lady." I waited until the door slid shut behind her, then turned to glare pointedly at John. "For the last time, John, are you with me?"

He looked from one to another of us, and I could see the bitter turmoil that raged within his soul. "I suppose I've come too far to let it go on without me," he said finally. "Count me in, but may God forgive us all."

"He will," I smiled. "Don't worry. Now, gentlemen, pay close attention, for this is how we plan to strike . . ."

Chapter Eight

Nothing can'st thou to damnation add
Greater than that.
～～～Othello～～～

Paine cleared a path through the crowd. Or, more precisely, the crowd made way for Lewis Paine. Lewis had a certain subtleness about him, somewhat akin to a locomotive, and I had yet to see his way impeded on any thoroughfare.

Davey and I made our way close behind Lewis, an admittedly odd parade in the fading twilight. We followed his lumbering, gray-swathed frame along Pennsylvania Avenue, and then across the muddy expanse of open field known as Lafayette Park, until we found ourselves herded amongst the rest of the fools who were milling towards the White House. Nearly four or five hundred had already gathered, and the rest of the streets surrounding the demon's lair were teeming with countless more. Word had spread that Lincoln was to give a victory speech, the first since news of the war's end had arrived, and for some unfathomable reason, over which I still struggled anxiously, I felt compelled to go. Perhaps it was simply because I wanted to hear what mindless drivel the Original Gorilla might have been prompted to say, considering he would soon be silenced. Forever.

I had lingered at the widow's until late evening. Once our business was completed, Davey, Lewis and I had joined the Surratts for supper. George had been tactfully banished, at Anna's fervent insistence, and it was while sharing the widow's meager but delicious fare that one of her boarders had returned with the news of the president's coming address. John had refused to go with us, retreating to his room in sullen silence, but Davey and Lewis were more than eager. I was growing increasingly worried over John. His demeanor had failed to grow any less cheerless as the evening had progressed. I wanted to speak to him, to try and bolster his spirits for our coming venture. Yet it was difficult to voice my concerns, in the company of his mother and Anna, so I held my tongue and promised myself to talk to him later. After a fine desert of apple dumplings and coffee, Lewis, Davey, and I took our gracious leave of the ladies and went out to see Old Abe.

An incredibly inept brass band, clad in the blue twill uniforms of the city Fire Department, struck up "The Battle Cry of Freedom" as we approached the ornate columns of the south portico. Hundreds of cheering voices took up the wretched song, while dozens of mischievous brats scampered trough the crowd, waving tiny flags and launching roman candles at unsuspecting victims. A pair of such urchins nearly bowled me over, practically setting my coat afire with their sparklers, but a cold glare from Lewis made both miscreants drop their fireworks and run screaming back to mama. Truly, the giant's talents were legion.

Davey pointed to a spreading magnolia tree that stood less than a hundred feet from the balcony where Lincoln was fond of speaking. The three of us made our way through an impromptu choral, most of whom were half-drunk, considering the slurred lyrics. Lewis shoved one boisterous virtuoso aside, and none too gently, but the man merely hiccoughed and resumed his song, along with a jubilant shout of "God bless the Union!" I refrained from smashing my cane across his grinning face, but just barely.

We stepped in under the flowering limbs, and discovered we had a tolerable view, despite the thickening crowd. I leaned against the massive trunk and savored the pleasant fragrance, which was actually something of a godsend. The wind was blowing from the south, and carrying the stench from the

Potomac Flats, a fetid marsh near the river that was directly across the White House lawn. I was distinctly pleased that Old Abe had this heady bouquet to wake up to every morning.

Davey glanced around speculatively. "Lots of folks out tonight."

"A lot of fools, you mean." I tugged a pint bottle of brandy, purchased along our trek, from my coat pocket. "Mindless sheep, every goddamn one of them." I threw a sullen look about me, draining the flask in two swift pulls. I thought I heard my name called out, once or twice, but I was in no mood to return the salutations. As I studied the mammoth crowd, I suddenly drew in my breath, certain for an anxious moment that I had recognized the ominous bulk of Luther Baker. Yet when I looked again, there was nothing, save for a chattering gaggle of Washington matrons. I tossed the bottle aside with an angry sigh. That bastard would undoubtedly haunt my very dreams.

The balcony door swung open, accompanied by a sudden tremendous roar from the crowd. But it swiftly died away, in a groan of disappointment, when the figure that emerged turned out to be a White House servant. The plucky fellow enjoyed his brief acclaim, however, bowing elegantly before he turned up the gaslights on either side of the double doors and slipped back inside. Another man then emerged, though the mob warily held its applause, and he nodded curtly to the firehouse band down below. A brass-helmeted conductor waved his baton, and the first hiccoughing notes of "Hail to the Chief" suddenly blared forth. A few seconds later, both balcony doors flew wide, and the Original Gorilla himself, Abraham Lincoln, stepped out onto the porch with a grinning wave.

I had never heard such a monstrous roar. Not even when the bastard had accepted the nomination, for a second miserable term, three months before. The crowd went absolutely insane, screaming and shouting at the top of raucous lungs, and the very ground beneath our feet seemed to tremble.

"Lincoln! Lincoln! Lincoln! Lincoln!"

The name was echoed, like some vile litany, over and over again, while Lincoln merely stood silent and smiled benevolently. I studied his lined, incredibly ugly face, in the flickering lamplight, and felt my anger begin to soar. He was here before me. The monster of the Union. The destroyer of the Confederacy. The very embodiment of all that was evil to the South. God, but the hatred that spilled over within my soul was nearly unbearable. All I could think of was the bargain I had made with Stanton, and how fervently I wished that I might be able to carry out the plan right then and there. I even found my hand slipping towards my coat pocket, where Prudy's gun still lay nestled, but I checked myself abruptly. All in good time, I mused, forcing my temper aside. All in damnably good time.

A small boy appeared on the balcony, clad in a miniature Yankee uniform. I took him to be the president's youngest son, Tad, judging from the way he capered freely about Lincoln's long legs. Lincoln reached down and scooped the child into gawky arms, and the two of them waved together, much to the enraptured delight of the mad fools below. Lincoln set the boy down, then waved both hands for silence.

It was several minutes in coming, but when it finally settled about us, along with the rapid nightfall, Lincoln lowered his hands.

"Good people," he called out, in that godawful squeak of a voice, "the war is over. Our great nation is whole once again."

Another roar sounded, as equally deafening as the first, though Lincoln quickly signaled for silence.

"You will join me, I beg you, in remembering the countless brave men of both sides who gave their lives for that which they honestly believed."

He bowed his bearded head, along with most of the crowd,

and what had once been sheer pandemonium was suddenly an eerie silence. I clenched my fists in rising fury.

"That hypocritical bastard," I whispered tersely to Paine. "God, if I only had a bigger gun."

Lewis reached inside his overcoat. "Here you go, Cap'n," he said flatly. "Take mine."

"Lewis, no!" I grabbed at his arm, glancing around frantically as I forced him to holster the LeMat. "Jesus Christ!" I hissed. "It's only a figure of speech!"

Paine shrugged his broad shoulders. "If you say so." His torpid eyes held a curious frown. "Just let me know if you change your mind."

I shook my head with a trembling sigh, coldly admonishing myself to guard my speech around the witless giant. I looked around once more, to make certain no one else had witnessed the near-catastrophe, but all eyes were fixed piously on the ground or the president.

Lincoln concluded his pharisaical prayer, and then began a garrulous speech about reunification, healing, and God knows how many other lies. In all honesty, I paid little attention to his words, for I had suddenly found the entire event far too vexing to bear. It was only when I heard the word Negroes that I bothered to listen once more. And keenly.

"The question has been raised," Lincoln sighed, as he leaned wearily against the iron balustrade, "as to the future of our Negro brethren, now that their chains have finally been struck off. In truth, it is a difficult issue to settle, and one that has no simple answers. Yet it must be stressed that the Negro has proven himself in battle, far beyond any question of loyalty or valor, and, as a consequence, must be considered an equal, at least in the eyes of his fellow white soldiers. For that reason, I believe it is fitting that the right to vote should be extended to those brave men of color who wore their country's uniform . . ."

"My God!" I heard myself rasp. "Stanton was right."

Davey Herold turned to frown at me. "Who was right, Mr. Booth?"

I shook my head quickly. "Nothing, Davey. Never mind." Yet I had to press my hands against my face as I struggled to maintain my composure. There was no longer any question as to the necessity of our enterprise, nor to the rationale of Stanton's extraordinary bargain. The Original Gorilla had damned himself with his very words. And I was absolutely certain of what I had to do.

Lincoln finished his obscene address, standing up straight to wave towards the band. "You fellows played some fine music tonight, but I think it's time we heard a different tune around here. I've always been sort of partial to the tune 'Dixie', and since the Attorney General has assured me that it belongs to the Union once again, I believe I'd like to hear it played right here in the Capital. Boys?"

I could not stand anymore. I prodded Lewis and Davey with my cane, angrily urging them to follow me away from the tree and through the cheering crowd. As the band struck up the Southern anthem, a filthy sacrilege in itself, I stalked away, ignoring both the age and gender of those I callously pushed aside. It wasn't until I reached the big statue of Andrew Jackson, in the middle of Lafayette Park, that I turned to wait for Lewis and Davey.

Davey hurried across the field, shaking his head anxiously as he and Paine trotted up to me. "Are you all right, Mr. Booth?"

"Oh, I'm just fine, Davey," I said through my teeth. I waved the walking stick towards the glimmering White House. "But that bastard certainly isn't, not by a damn sight! I intend to put him through!" I glared at both of them, before turning away to head back to the National. "Mark my words, gentlemen, that's the last goddamn speech Mr. Lincoln will ever make!"

Chapter Nine

If this were played upon a stage now,
I could condemn it as improbable fiction.
~~~Twelfth Night~~~

Granbury, Texas - September, 1876

"Fetch me a drink of water, would you, Finis?" St. Helen paused in his incredible story, waving a trembling hand at a pitcher near his bed. "Finis?"

"What? Oh, yes, water!" I shook myself out of my mesmerized stupor. "Of course, John, of course. My God!" My own hand quavered as I poured him a drink. "I've never heard anything so . . . so . . ."

"Unbelievable?" St. Helen smiled over the glass I held for him, dark eyes fixed grimly on mine. "Yes," he said when he'd finished drinking. "I suppose it does sound fantastic. But it's true, Finis. All of it."

"You are John Wilkes Booth?" I set the glass aside and sat back in my chair. "For God's sake, John, how can this be? Booth is dead. He was killed in some barn in Virginia. The entire world knows that!"

He chuckled at that, genuinely bemused. "There are more things in heaven and earth, Horatio. Never believe all you hear, Finis. As a lawyer, you should know that."

"But how—"

St. Helen suddenly began to shiver, violently, as if a cold chill had swept through the room. I hurriedly tugged the blankets about his body and waited anxiously for the spasm to pass. He gasped for breath, after a few uncertain minutes, then his eyes fluttered open and he forced a wan smile. "Perhaps you should fetch the medicine Dr. Ellis prescribed?"

"Immediately!" I fairly dashed out of the bedroom and snatched up the bottle that Ellis had left on the hall table. St. Helen gulped a sizable portion, once I returned, and his baleful quivering seemed to subside almost instantly. He nodded his thanks.

"Malaria," he croaked. "I've had it before, but never quite this bad. I'm afraid I may not last the night, Finis."

"Nonsense," I said, forcing a plucky smile, though secretly I feared he may have been right. "Why don't you try and get some sleep, John?"

"No!" He shook his head vehemently. "I can't die until I've rid my conscience of this guilt! I will shortly stand before the gates of Judgment, Finis, and I want the Almighty to know that I tried. Please." He waved me back towards my chair. "At least let me speak while I still can."

I sat down once again. "John, listen to me. It is not possible that you are John Wilkes Booth. For one thing, there were witnesses to Booth's death. And for another, you say that Stanton told you that if Lincoln died the South would not suffer. And yet—"

"And yet she suffered quite wretchedly," he finished with a mournful sigh. "Yes, Finis, I am painfully aware of what befell our dear country. My whole life has been a semblance of that suffering. I visited the South, in the years following the war. Atlanta, Vicksburg, I've seen them all. And I was the one who caused their pain. Yes, me," he said to my skeptic frown. "And as far as my death is concerned, let me assure you, Finis, a man can die in many different ways . . ."

Chapter Ten

I am betrayed by keeping company
With men like you; men of inconsistency.
                     ~~~Julius Caesar~~~

Washington, D.C. - April, 1865

Good Friday morning dawned humidly gray and oppressive, as if Nature itself was aware of our coming enterprise. I rose early and dressed in my finest suit, then made my way out of the National and traversed the short distance to Wood's Barber Shop. I paused along E Street to cast a furtive glance or two for Luther Baker, but it was more out of anxious rote than real suspicion. The past few days, since the night of Lincoln's speech, I had caught no further sight of the giant, a fact for which I was both grateful and perturbed. Yet I had no time to worry about being dogged, for the plans for tonight's performance took precedence over all.

The details were perfected; every man knew his role. Lewis was to accompany me, guarding my back should any unforeseen champion try to defend Old Abe. George was to ready his boat; Davey to wait outside the theater with the horses. And John, who still displayed his bitter reluctance in every line of his body, was to guide us all out of Washington City and down the Maryland peninsula, to the safety of a courier's hideout somewhere within the Virginia tidewater. From there we would board a small Confederate sloop which would ferry us quickly to Canada, and from thence, God alone knew. The only item still missing was the stage for our play, or, more precisely, the theater, but I had no reason to doubt that Stanton would keep his end of the bargain in that respect. What truly plagued me, as it had from the very night this wretched business began, was whether he would honor the remainder of his covenant. I had yet to hear from Jacob Thompson in Montreal, and I could hardly storm into the War Department and demand to know the whereabouts of my promised funds. I had little choice but to trust the Yankee bastard, an irony which caused me no end of bitter chagrin.

After I left Wood's, smelling keenly of bay rum and apple pomade, I walked down Tenth Street to the huge red brick edifice of Ford's Theater.

John Ford had bought the former Baptist church two years previously, ignoring an angry congregationist's curse that nothing good would ever come of the place once it became a haven for heathen actors. How well it had served as a church I couldn't say, but it was definitely a grand theater. I had performed there many times, and always to packed houses. Ford's served as my mailing address, as it did for most actors when in residence in Washington, and I wanted to see, as I had for the past three interminable days, if there might be some news from Canada.

I passed Peter Taltuval's Star Saloon, which stood just next door to Ford's, and resisted the sudden urge to quench my thirst. I needed all my wits about me this day, and reluctantly pushed the savored notion of a brandy constitutional out of my thoughts.

Harry Ford, the younger brother of the theater's owner, was standing outside the front entrance with two men who were unknown to me. Harry was a lanky youth, barely twenty-one, with brown eyes and a shock of curly dark hair. Harry managed the place, and did a competent job, considering his age, but he fancied himself an actor. Unfortunately, his talent was woefully limited to bookkeeping. I saw him turn as I approached, gleefully taking in my top hat and walking stick.

"Behold, gentlemen," Harry grinned to his companions

with a wave in my direction. "The dandiest man in Washington!" He held out a thin hand. "Wilkes, good to see you again. How long has it been, anyway? An entire day?"

I returned the smile, but not the handshake. "Your wit matches your acting ability, Harry. Exceedingly thin. Any mail for me today?"

He never lost his broad smirk. "As a matter of fact, there is. I was hoping you'd stop by and collect it, so as to stop bothering me."

"Harry, the only time anyone bothers you is when you hand out the pay envelopes. You could hire a nigger to take your place and no one would know the difference."

I saw him flinch a little at that, especially when his friends chortled jovially, but Harry kept his pluck. "Very funny, Booth. You'll have to tell me from what fellow actor you stole that line. Come along inside." He nodded to the two men, and I followed him through the ornate lobby and into the theater office.

Harry pulled a small stack of envelopes from a pigeonhole rack behind his cluttered desk. "For you, my dear Mr. Booth. And please don't be overly generous with your thanks."

"Don't worry," I smiled as I took the letters. "I won't." The topmost envelope bore a return address of Bel Air, and I recognized my mother's stilted handwriting. I had meant to write her a note of my own, as it had been far too long since I'd been home for a visit. And after tonight . . . I shoved the letter into a coat pocket and brushed the dismal thought aside. The next two were inconsequential—notes from female admirers, judging from the perfumed scent—but the neatly printed letters on the last envelope fairly leapt off the wrinkled paper, especially the word Montreal. I ripped it open and quickly read through the single-page note.

"*. . . Inform you of an unusually large deposit of two hundred fifty thousand dollars . . .*"

"Good news?" Harry asked suddenly, undoubtedly prompted by the huge grin that had suddenly contorted my face.

"Extremely good news," I chirped.

"Well, then." Harry smiled in return. "Perhaps you'd like to hear some more?"

I nodded absently, rereading the incredible letter. My hands had started an uncontrollable quaking. "Of course, Harry, of course."

"President Lincoln will be attending tonight's performance, along with General Grant himself."

My shaking hands went abruptly still. I looked up at Harry. "Lincoln and Grant? Here?"

He nodded proudly. "John had me send out the invitations this morning. Seems Laura Keene's celebrating her thousandth performance in Cousin tonight. John wants to make it a special celebration, sort of a gift to Laura, especially since attendance has been down. He figures having Lincoln and Grant here might pack the house."

I felt my pulse quicken. "Has Lincoln replied?"

"Not yet, but I doubt he'll miss it." Harry studied me with a sly grin. "You know they'll have General Lee with them, don't you? I plan to set 'em up in opposite boxes, so the folks can get a good look." He spread both hands. "The winners on the right, and the losers on the left. What do you think, Wilkes?"

I found little humor in his jest, and let him know with my glare. "I doubt even the Yankees would parade their captives like Roman conquerors, especially a man like General Lee. Tell me, though, when do you think you'll know for certain that Lincoln is coming?"

He shrugged. "John's already got the stagehands fixing up the presidential box, so I reckon he's pretty certain. But I suppose the official reply won't come back till this afternoon. Why do you ask?"

"What? Oh, no reason." I folded Thompson's telegram and tucked it into my pocket. "Just curious. Thanks for holding my mail, Harry."

Harry chuckled ruefully. "Anytime, Wilkes. Anytime."

I hurried out of Ford's and down the street, anxiously heading for the Kirkwood Hotel. Harry's news was both good and bad. The fact that Lincoln would be attending was the good, since I knew the theater inside and out. But if Grant was to accompany him, then God only knew how easily I could approach the president, since the bastard general had his own cadre of bodyguards. It was doubtful that even Stanton could order them away. I had to get a message to the Secretary as quickly as possible.

The Kirkwood stood on Pennsylvania Avenue just east of the White House. It was far smaller than the National, but it had a devoted clientele, mostly Union officials who found its location convenient. Including the Vice-President of the United States.

I stepped inside the Kirkwood's unobtrusive lobby and swiftly approached the desk, where I asked a bespectacled young clerk for pen and paper. Quickly, I penned a brief note on a sheet of hotel stationary.

"Lincoln attending Ford's this p.m. Grant supposed to be with him. Need instructions as to next steps. J.W.B."

I folded the note, slipped it inside the accompanying envelope, then scribbled the vice-president's name across the front.

"Don't wish to disturb you." I scrawled under Johnson's name. *"Are you at home?"*

Handing the note to the clerk, who fervently promised to see that it was delivered, I turned to leave the hotel. Almost immediately, I collided with an immovable colossus that turned out to be a man.

"Pardon me, friend," I said curtly. "Why the hell don't you

watch—" The remainder of my snarled reproach trailed off in a horrified gasp, as I lifted my eyes to the giant.

"You need to come with me, Reb," Luther Baker said quietly. He swept his contemptuous sneer past me, at the five or six unassuming patrons who loitered in the lobby, waiting until their attention was no longer drawn to us. Then he tossed his big head towards a curtained doorway not far from the desk. "This way." To punctuate the growled command, he slipped aside his coat to reveal his gun.

I followed him dutifully, as a cold sweat began to trickle down my spine, down a narrow hallway from which a number of small storerooms opened off. Luther suddenly pointed into one of them, and I made no attempt to refuse his direction. I stepped inside, alone, and he swiftly closed the door behind me.

The room was rank with the smell of mildew and must. There were several tall shelves, heaped with yellowed sheets and draperies, and the only light came from a small window set high in the back wall. For a single moment, I had the terrified impression of a prison cell, and the first waves of claustrophobic panic were just beginning to nip at me when a small but familiar figure stepped out from behind one of the shelves.

"Please forgive me, Mr. Booth, but this was the only manner I could arrange for us to meet, given such short notice."

I sighed in fervent relief. "Truly, Mr. Stanton, the theater is distinctly poorer without your talent for melodrama. I have rarely felt this anxious."

"Circumstance compels my actions," he said curtly. "There has been a slight change of plans."

"I know. I have just come from Ford's to leave you the message. General Grant is attending the play with Mr. Lincoln."

Stanton scowled at me vexedly. "No, Mr. Booth, that is not the change to which I refer. I can assure you, sir, Grant will not be accompanying the president. I have already convinced the general that it is in his best interests to leave Washington, this very night, as the city is still rife with dangerous radicals. Besides, Mrs. Grant hates Mrs. Lincoln with a passion, so the persuasion was not at all difficult."

I blinked in confusion. "But if Grant is not to be there, then why the concern?"

Stanton tugged at his small fingers, shrugging coyly as he met my guarded stare. "It is difficult to fully explain. There are a number of government officials who have become, shall we say, suspicious of my actions. They are closely allied to Mr. Lincoln, and do not share my inclinations in this matter. They could very easily compromise the entire situation. As a consequence, I must ask you to alter your plans."

"Alter? In what way?"

He turned away, pacing the narrow space between the shelves and the storeroom wall. "Lincoln's death must appear to be the work of organized subversives. It must have the appearance of a disruption; an attempt by Southern sympathizers to confound the government. Only by this confusion can the individuals responsible assume total control." He stopped to frown up at me. "Do you understand, Mr. Booth?"

My temper rapidly began to surge. "You want to make it appear that Jefferson Davis arranged the assassination," I said heatedly. "Is this so you can make it all the easier to hang him?"

"Davis won't hang," Stanton insisted. "I promise you, Mr. Booth, none of the Southern leaders will be harmed. Not if Lincoln dies. But once he is dead, there has to be a diversion, some manner by which key personages can step in. And for this I need your assistance."

My anger was quickly replaced by a rising trepidation. "How?"

Stanton held up two fingers. "There must be assassination

attempts made on the lives of two other government officials. Secretary of State Seward, and Vice-President Johnson."

"Jesus Christ!" My horrified reel backwards was halted only by a rickety shelf. "I thought you said Johnson was a puppet! Now you want me to kill him as well?"

The Secretary waved anxious hands. "Calm yourself, Mr. Booth. I said attempts, that's all. Just attempts. I am not asking you to kill the Vice-President. Nor Seward, for that matter. The Secretary of State is laid up at home from a carriage accident. You could merely fire a bullet through his window. Johnson will be right here in the hotel. Surely one of your confederates can effect some perfunctory assailment?"

"My confederates, as you call them, were scarcely able to commit themselves to this entire affair! They already believe me to be out of my mind! In God's Name, Mr. Stanton . . ." I drew away from him, as far as the shelves would permit. "What is this truly all about? This has nothing to do with salvaging the South, has it, sir?"

In the cold gleam of his dark eyes, I saw my answer. He shook his gray head slowly. "Truly, sir, that question is not yours to ask. As I recall, I am paying you, and quite handsomely, for your participation."

"The hell with your goddamned money!" I pulled Thompson's telegram from my pocket and threw it at his feet. "No amount is worth any of this devil's madness! Take it, sir," I hissed at him. "Take it and be damned!"

The Secretary sighed, calmly stooping to retrieve the paper. "I don't think I need to remind you of what is truly at stake here, Mr. Booth. Events have already been set into motion which cannot be halted. If you wish to renege on our agreement, then so be it. But keep in mind, yours will not be the only life that is forfeit."

I held his glare, contemptuously. "My comrades are not afraid to die for what they believe in!"

"Indeed? And is that also true of the woman?"

An iron fist seemed to suddenly plunge into my gut. "What?"

"The woman, Mr. Booth," Stanton repeated flatly. "I believe her name is . . . Surratt? Is she, too, prepared to give her life for your cause?"

"Give her life . . ?" I could barely croak the words, let alone fathom their meaning. "My God, sir, you wouldn't . . . Christ Almighty, she has nothing to do with this!"

"She's a traitor, sir. She owns the house where you and your associates meet. Her own son is one of your plotters. I don't need any more evidence than that." He pursed his lips, pensively. "She has a daughter, too, as I recall. Quite lovely, according to Lieutenant Baker. Perhaps she, too, is a member of your nefarious league?"

"Dear God!" The little room began a hellish spin. I clutched at a shelf, fighting to maintain what tenuous hold on sanity I still possessed. "You contemptible bastard! How could you do this? How could you possibly do this?"

"Me?" His dark eyes never flickered. "Their lives are in your hands. Not mine"

"All right." Slowly, painfully, I nodded in resignation. "All right, God damn you! I'll do as you ask!"

"To be honest, Mr. Booth," Stanton said dryly, "I never had the slightest doubt that you would. Now, tell me, how do plan to leave Washington City?"

"By the Navy Yard Bridge," I shrugged, bleakly. "Then south through Maryland."

The Secretary nodded thoughtfully. "Towards Bryantown?"

"Yes. By way of the T.B. Road."

"Then that shall be your password. When you reach the bridge, just say 'T.B. Road' to the officer on guard. He'll let you pass through." Stanton edged past me, then paused at the door. "Please don't take any of this personally, Mr. Booth.

Everything I have done has been for a reason. This entire situation is far greater than you or I put together. It might even be argued that Providence itself lends a guiding hand."

I could not meet his wretched gaze. "Go to hell."

The bastard merely shrugged, then reached into his pocket and slowly withdrew a different slip of paper. "Here," he said as he held it out to me. "Just to let you know I am not a man without some consideration."

I took the paper, which I could see was another telegram, and opened it with trembling hands.

"A second dispatch from your friend Mr. Thompson," Stanton offered. "It arrived this morning, and I had it intercepted before it could be delivered to Ford's. I wanted to give it to you personally."

Frowning, I read the message, and a single line stood out from all the rest.

". . . for a total deposit of six hundred thousand dollars . . ."

"Jesus!" The words, and the room, suddenly went blurred before my eyes.

Stanton tapped at the door, and a brief moment later Luther pushed it open. The Secretary started to step through, then stopped abruptly and turned to face me. "From this moment on, Mr. Booth, you will do exactly as I have directed. You will make no attempts to warn any of your companions, including the woman, and neither will you make any attempt to run. If you violate any of these agreements, and believe me, I will know if you do, then God alone will have to take mercy on you. I myself will have none. Good day to you, sir."

I waited until the door closed behind him, and the room went deathly silent, before I slowly sank to my knees and surrendered to a flood of ungovernable tears.

Chapter Eleven

For 'tis sport to have the engineer
Hoist with his own petard.
~~~Hamlet~~~

"What's all this about, Cap'n?"

Lewis Paine sat near the door with his long, powerful legs stretched out before him. He eyed me with only the slightest glimmer of curiosity in those mysterious blue eyes. "I thought we was all primed for tonight?"

"We were, Lewis." I met his laconic gaze for a single bleak moment, before turning to stare back out the window of my hotel room. I watched as a squadron of Yankee cavalry paraded triumphantly below. "We bloody well were."

"You lucky, Mr. Booth," George Atzerodt hiccoughed. He lolled in the armchair, where I had tersely ordered him after he tried to sprawl across my bed. "I almost leave for Port Tobacco before you find me."

"Marvelous, George," I sneered as I closed the curtain. "You'll never know how grateful I am."

I turned to scowl at both of them. It had taken me nearly two hours, once I had finally been able to leave that miserable storeroom, to track each of them down. I found Lewis in his drab room at the Herndon House Hotel, which he kept at my expense. George was in a tavern, as usual, and considering the rate at which he was consuming his cheap gin, I seriously doubted he would have been capable of traveling anywhere. Davey was at work in Thompson's Apothecary, and I had sent him to fetch John and then meet the rest of us back at the National. I myself could not, under any circumstance, deign to go near the widow's. Not today. Nor ever again.

My God, but I was a fool. The Yankees had fashioned their

snare, and in my damnable arrogance, my pathetic peacock's strut, I had blithely stepped inside. I had fallen for Stanton's insidious ruse just like one of my giddy virgins, and for the first time in my life, I understood their tears of betrayal. The great John Booth—Confederate savior, slayer of tyrants, righter of all Southern wrongs—was nothing more than a loathsome puppet, dangling from hangman's cords. And the tune to which I danced my obsequious jig was Yankee Doodle. Shakespeare himself could hardly have penned such magnificent irony.

"What's so funny, Mr. Booth?"

I gaped at Paine's puzzled query. "What?"

"You was smilin'," he said with a yawn. "Reckon you must have thought of a good joke."

"Oh, it's a grand joke, Lewis," I said bitterly. "And I'm the goddamn butt!"

"How's that?"

I shook my head swiftly, as a brief knock suddenly sounded. "Never mind. Just get the door."

Paine had his LeMat swiftly palmed by the time he cracked the door and peered out. He loosed a guttural grunt, then stepped back as John and Davey quickly stepped inside.

John glanced around nervously, then fixed his sullen frown on me. "What's going on, Wilkes? I was in the middle of important business when Davey showed up."

"It can't be helped," I said quickly. "There's been a change in our plans, and I had to see all of you immediately."

"A change?" He didn't care for the sound of that, and in all honesty, I couldn't blame him. "What kind of change?"

I had difficulty in forming the words. And meeting his eyes. "There have been . . . new developments. We have to make an attempt on Secretary of State Seward and the Vice-President, as well as Lincoln."

Slowly, John began to laugh; a sniggering chortle that

matched his look of bewilderment. He glanced about at the others, who shared the same befuddled stares. "Truly, Wilkes," John said as he turned back to me. "For an actor, you have a propensity for poor jests."

"We don't have to kill them," I continued, ignoring his growing confusion. "Just make it appear that they were part of the original plan."

"What plan?" John swiftly lost his baffled grin. "What the hell is this all about? First you tell us we're to kill the president, and at someone else's beckoning. Now we're to assault Seward and Johnson as well?" He shook his dark head angrily. "No, Wilkes, not me! I want no part of this whole bloody business. You were mad to think I'd even go along in the first place!"

"John, please." I was trembling in such desperate anguish I could barely stand. "You don't understand! We have no choice in—"

"You have no choice!" he suddenly roared. "You, Wilkes! This is your insanity, not mine!" he waved a finger around the room, with a red-faced glower at all of us. "If the rest of these bastards want to follow you to hell, that's their affair! But not me! I've been a part of this goddamn madness for too long! I'll have no more, do you understand? No more!" He spun on his heel and stalked towards the door.

"John, wait!" I fairly leaped in front of him, grabbing at his coat lapels. "For God's sake, listen to me! You can't run!" I shook him frantically, nearly in tears once again. "None of us can run! None of us!"

He pushed me away with a scowl of disgust. "Get your goddamned hands off of me! I can damn well do as I please, and no man can stop me!"

"They know about us!" I wailed desperately. "They know about the kidnap plot, where we've met, everything! If we try to run, they'll hang us all!" I met his livid gaze pleadingly.

"They'll hang your mother and Anna . . ."

"Mother and Anna?" He blinked at me, shaking his head. "Why in hell would they hang mother and Anna?"

"Because that's the kind of demons they are," I sighed dolefully. "And there's not a goddamn thing we can do about it. Except to do exactly as they say."

John looked around the room again, then suddenly pushed past me. "I don't believe you!"

I grabbed at him again. "John, please—"

I wasn't prepared for the fist that suddenly slammed against my jaw. By the time I recovered, crawling to my knees from the carpeted floor, Lewis had one huge hand wrapped around John's throat, while the other held a glittering dagger to the side of Surratt's terrified face. Davey and George could only watch the incredulous scene in slack-jawed horror.

"Let him go, Lewis," I said as I staggered to my feet.

Paine frowned at me sharply. "You sure you don't want me to kill him, Cap'n?"

I shook my head, rubbing a hand at the throbbing pain. "Just let him go."

Paine complied, reluctantly, and John swiftly backed away, brushing at his clothes indignantly as he glared from the giant to me. "I'm leaving, Wilkes. I'm leaving Washington City, tonight, and you're not going to stop me."

"Where do you plan to go?"

He shrugged. "Canada. I have friends there, just like you."

I eyed him grimly. "What about your mother, John? Don't you give a damn about her? Or Anna?"

He rolled his dark eyes. "Don't be a fool, Wilkes! Not even the Yankees would be brutal enough to hang women." He reached for the door, then turned to stare back at me forlornly. "Poor Wilkes. What an incredibly pathetic creature you've become. And to think that I actually used to admire you." He turned the same dismal look to the others, then swiftly left the room.

"God damn it!" I slammed a fist against the door. "What about you," I demanded, turning back to glare at the others. "Do you want to leave, as well?"

Paine slid his dagger into a sheath beneath his coat. "Ain't got nowhere else to go, Cap'n," he said with his sneering grin. "Might as well stick with you. George'll stay, too." He flicked his blue eyes to the cowering German. "Won't you, George?"

Atzerodt slowly, mournfully nodded. "*Ja*, I stay too."

I looked at Davey, who swiftly lit up with his perpetual grin. "Don't even have to ask, Mr. Booth."

I nodded my appreciation. "I wish it could be different, gentlemen, but I suppose we'll simply have to make the best of things. And I'm afraid our plans for tonight will have to be modified. Lewis, do you know where Secretary Seward lives?"

He shook his big head. "'Fraid not, Cap'n."

"What about you, Davey?"

"Sure," the boy shrugged. "Over on Fifteenth, near the White House."

"Fine. You take Lewis over there tonight, around ten o'clock. Wait outside while Lewis goes in and . . ." I drew in my breath, ". . . tries to shoot at Seward."

Paine studied me queerly. "You don't want me to kill him?"

"No! For God's sake, just pretend that's what you've come to do! Fire into the wall, the floor, whatever! Just don't kill the bastard!"

Paine nodded, slowly, but I could see a look of genuine disappointment in his taciturn stare. "How do I get inside?"

I thought for a moment. "Seward was in an accident, so I suppose he'll be on medication. Davey, take along some sort of remedy from Thompson's. Lewis can tell Seward's servants he's there with a prescription. Lewis, once you've scared the wits out of the bastard, you and Davey ride like hell for Lloyd's Tavern. Wait there for me. And don't forget; when you get to the Navy Yard Bridge, tell the guard who challenges you 'T.B. Road'. Do you understand? T.B. Road."

They both repeated the password, and I turned to Atzerodt. "George, you will go over to the Kirkwood Hotel, and I know damn well you know where that's at, since you've undoubtedly gotten drunk in their taproom. At ten o'clock, you will walk upstairs to Vice-President Johnson's room, knock on the door, and when the son of a bitch opens up, you will take out your gun and fire over his head. Is that clear?"

"But I stay with boat!" He whined like a petulant child. "You say I stay with boat, Mr. Booth!"

"That was before," I sighed. "Now you have a different job."

He shook his mangy head rapidly, and I was certain he was ready to start blubbering. "But you say I stay with boat! I don't want to kill nobody!"

"Damn it, George!" I hauled him up out of the chair, none too gently, and slammed him hard against the wall. "I don't give a damn what I told you! You don't have to kill anyone! Just knock on his goddamn door, take out your goddamn gun, and fire over his goddamn head! Do you understand me?"

The look in his bloodshot eyes was close to panic. "*Ja, ja,* I understand! I shoot over his head!" He leered at me piteously. "Then I go to boat, Mr. Booth?"

I let go of his filthy coat. "Yes, George, then you can go to your goddamned boat. But I swear to you, if you fail me in this, then I'll hand you over to Lewis."

The German rolled his eyes to a smugly grinning Paine, then nodded anxiously at me. "I don't fail you, Mr. Booth!"

"And remember the password!"

"*Ja*, T.B. Road! I remember!"

I turned away from all of them, pressing my hands against my face. "Get out, now. All of you. I'll see you tonight in Surrattsville."

The door opened, and I heard them slowly shuffle out. All

except for Davey, who gently slipped his hand on my shoulder. "You reckon you'll be all right, Mr. Booth?"

"I'll be fine, Davey. Thanks for asking."

"Don't be too mad at John," he said quietly. "Reckon he's just scared."

I nodded, grudgingly. "He has a right to be. I wish to God we could all run with him."

Davey frowned up at me thoughtfully. "You really think we should do this, Mr. Booth? Kill Mr. Lincoln, that is?"

"We no longer have any choice, Davey boy. Not anymore. But don't you worry." I gave him my pluckiest grin. "I've a plan or two of my own for the bastards. You go on, now, and watch after Lewis. I'll see you at Lloyd's."

Once he had gone, I sat down at my desk and pulled a bottle of brandy from a drawer. It took several hearty swigs, but I finally summoned the courage I needed, then picked up my pen and quickly began to write. Edwin Stanton, I mused with a grim smile, might very well have written this filthy pageant. But as God was my witness, John Wilkes Booth would pen the finale.

Chapter Twelve

I cannot remember such things were
That were not precious to me.
<div align="center">~~~Macbeth~~~</div>

"Papa, dear," the woman chirped gaily, "here are letters for you. One for you, Mrs. Mountchessington, one for you, Captain DeBoots, and one for you Lieutenant Vernon."

The red-coated British naval officer, his youthful face eagerly aglow, hurried across the ornate drawing room and held out his hand. "Ah, one for me, Florence?"

The woman laughed, mischievously hiding the envelope behind her elegant dress. "Now, now, what will you give me for the letter, lieutenant?"

"Stop!"

A short, spindly, middle-aged man, clad in an outrageously archaic suit, suddenly bolted from the curtained wings and rushed towards the knot of puzzled actors. "For the love of God, Laura, how many times do I have to tell you? This scene works better if you face stage right!" He shook a bamboo cane towards the darkened auditorium. "The audience needs to see your face!"

Laura Keene spun fumingly around, both fists pressed hard against broad hips. "God damn it, Harry!" Her cultured British accent suddenly assumed an entirely unladylike tone. "I think I should bloody well know which direction to face! I've been performing in this damned play longer than I care to remember!"

Harry Hawk rolled his dark eyes mournfully. "As have I, my dear, as have I. And one would think we would both have the good sense to find another. But unless and until we do, you have to face stage right!"

A roar of laughter erupted from the theater wings, and included my own. Laura Keene guffawed uproariously, along with the others, and Billy Ferguson, the young actor portraying Lt. Vernon, had difficulty resuming his military bearing.

Harry waved his hands in obvious defeat. "All right, people, dinner break. And don't take all night. I should like to finish this bloody rehearsal in my own lifetime."

I stepped behind the prompter's desk as the cast of "Our American Cousin" hurried off of Ford's cavernous stage. The final dress rehearsal, for tonight's performance would end the perennial Washington run, was in full swing. I smiled and nodded to each player as they passed by, mumbling some trifling compliment or another. I knew nearly all of them, of course, including the British actors who were part of Laura Keene's private ensemble. The play, an overrated relic concerning an American heir to an English fortune, was Keene's personal project, and had been for the past several years. It was hardly surprising, since Laura, once considered a promising actress in her native England, had never fully blossomed following her American debut. A debut which had unfortunately coincided with my brother Edwin's. Now Laura's talent, and her looks, had sadly faded, and the mediocre comedy was all she truly had left.

Laura and Harry Hawk, who was also the stage manager, director, and who portrayed the celebrated cousin himself, were among the last to leave the stage. Laura turned curious eyes to mine as she drew near.

"Why, hello, John," she said affably. "I haven't seen you in quite some time. You're looking well."

I tipped my hat. "Laura. You're looking as rapturous as ever." It was a gracious lie, of course, for time had not been kind to the forty-year-old actress. She had once been beautiful, that much was obvious, with long auburn hair, blue eyes, and a figure that was still passably fetching. I myself had once succumbed to her ample charms, years before when I was younger and less discriminating. But the lines in her sagging face were now etched too far deeply, and even the heavy makeup she wore could no longer compensate.

Laura studied me candidly. "And how is Edwin, these days? I haven't seen him since he lost his wife. That was what, two years ago?"

"He is recovering from Mary's death," I nodded. "But I shall tell him you inquired."

She gathered up her flowing satin skirts. "Don't bother," she sniffed curtly. "I doubt he'd even be interested." Laura flounced away in a sudden huff.

"Just like a bloody elephant," Harry Hawk growled, shaking his graying head as he stepped up beside me. "She just won't forget!"

I shrugged gamely. "Don't worry about it, Harry. We're all temperamental bastards, you know that."

"It's still damned inconsiderate, Wilkes! It wasn't Edwin's fault that Laura's career foundered. His talent would overshadow anyone." Harry threw me a sudden sheepish grin. "Present company excluded, of course."

I managed a chuckle. "Of course. I understand you're ending your run tonight?"

"On our way to Philadelphia," he sighed. "Where we shall undoubtedly perform this miserable disaster another thousand times."

I clapped him on a gaunt shoulder. "Come now, Harry, you're the star! You have the funniest lines in the play."

"I have the only funny line in the play," he snorted cynically.

"Ah, yes," I nodded. "Third act, second scene, correct?"

His pinched face lit up in stark astonishment. "There! You see? Even you know how predictable the damned thing is!"

He lowered his voice, glancing around furtively. "The only reason we're even rehearsing is because her majesty wants tonight's performance to be her grandest. The President's coming, you know."

"So I'd heard."

Harry prodded me with his cane. "Tell you what, Wilkes. Why don't you trade places with me tonight? You get the laughs, and I'll sit out in the audience and catch a few well-deserved winks."

"Sorry, Harry." I glanced past him, at the huge flag-draped theater box that loomed above the right side of the stage. "I'm afraid I have a previous engagement this evening."

He nodded bleakly. "From which you'll probably gather significantly more pleasure than myself. Oh, well . . ." He tugged his watch from a vest pocket. "If you'll excuse me, Wilkes, I'm off to dinner. And if I'm judicious, I may get sufficiently drunk by the time the curtain rises."

Harry hustled on by, and I was left alone in the vast theater.

I walked calmly across the stage, my bootheels casting an eerie echo through the massive gallery. The theater was my home, my haven, my sanctum sanctorum, as it were, and it was breaking my heart to know that, after tonight, I would be forced to leave her forever. I stopped in center stage, glancing around at the papier-mache scenery and musty curtains, and then above, at the intricate tangle of ropes and pulleys and sandbags which controlled this magnificent world of make-believe. A world which, as far as I was concerned, was far more preferable to the one we knew as reality. Especially the reality which I had so callously created for myself.

"To be or not to be," I shouted to the empty auditorium. "That is the question! Whether 'tis nobler to be a champion or a craven coward . . ." I smiled at my bleak improvisation. "Yet wise enough to know the goddamn difference."

"Who's down there?"

I whirled in alarm at the shouted voice, slapping at my pocket for Prudy's little gun. A figure stood within the presidential box, hidden by dark shadows. I backed away as it loomed closer, groping for the derringer as a pair of rough hands slid over the bunting of Union flags on the railing. An even rougher face followed the hands, peering intently towards the stage. "Who is that? Is that you, John Wilkes?"

"Jesus, Ned!" I shook a trembling finger at the scowling face. "You scared the living hell out of me! I thought you were a ghost!"

"Ghosts don't like theaters, John Wilkes," Ned Spangler snorted. "They're too respectable for the sort of folks they have to commingle with. What're you doin' down there, anyways?"

I had to laugh, despite my sudden jolt. Ned Spangler was an old friend, and not just of mine. Old Ned was Ford's top stagehand, a carpenter of unparalleled skill, and had seemingly been around since Shakespeare. He and my father had been fast friends, and Ned had even worked on our rambling house in Bel Air. He had always called me John Wilkes, for as long as I could remember, save for those times when I was a mischievous brat who stole his tools. Then his appellations were far less admirable.

"Just returning to old haunts," I called jovially. "What are you about up there?"

Ned jerked a thumb over his stooped shoulder. "Me an' Peanut are puttin' on the dog for Old Abe." He pointed to a gilded portrait of George Washington that hung squarely between the divided sections of the box. "John an' Harry even had us hang out Mr. Washington, as you can see. 'Course, just twixt you an' me, John Wilkes, Abe Lincoln don't even belong in the same room as a good Virginian like George." Ned launched a stream of brown tobacco juice somewhere towards the orchestra pit. "Wouldn't you say so?"

"I have been known to share that opinion." I pointed

curiously to the box. "What all have you done?"

Ned shrugged, slapping at the upright beam to his right. "Took out the false wall, made the box bigger, for one thing. Gen'ral Grant is supposed to come along." He nodded towards a garishly upholstered red velvet chair just behind him. "Harry had me fetch his own rocking chair for Mr. Lincoln, good Republican boy that he is. Reckon he don't want Old Abe gettin' piles?"

"Could be," I laughed. "Tell me something, Ned, are the locks on those box doors still broken?"

He nodded, vexedly. "Yeah, I reckon they are. I keep meanin' to fix 'em, but there's always somethin' else comes along." He waved a leathery hand above his gray head. "This whole damned place would likely fall apart if it weren't for Peanut an' me!"

I pulled a ten-dollar gold piece from my pocket. "Here," I chuckled, flipping it the ten or twelve feet to his waiting grasp. "Why don't you and Peanut reward your diligence with a bottle over at Taltuval's? My treat."

Ned flashed a grateful grin. "John Wilkes, you're a credit to your father an' your profession! An' believe me, comin' from ol' Neddy, that's a compliment!" He glanced back towards the interior of the box. "Peanut, come an' say thank you to the great Mr. Booth."

A second figure slowly materialized in the opposite window; a tow-headed youth with a lopsided grin and constantly darting eyes. "Peanut" was really Joseph Burroughs, but garnered his nickname from his general occupation of selling peanuts and popcorn at Ford's front entrance. He was barely sixteen, if even that old, and decidedly simpleminded, but an industrious soul nonetheless. Peanut smiled down and waved at me, rubbing a filthy sleeve across his nose.

"Come on, boy," Ned said to him. "Let's go slake our thirst. I'll buy you a ginger-beer an' a boiled egg. John Wilkes," he called, waving the coin. "Sure you don't want to come along?"

"No thanks, Neddy. You two enjoy yourselves."

I watched the two of them exit the box and amble along the upper balcony, or dress circle, as it was called, until they disappeared through the narrow door at the back that led to the stairs. Once they were out of sight, I turned my attention back to the box.

It would be a simple affair, once the deed was done, to jump the short distance from the box to the stage. Such a feat was by no means rare to me, as a number of my critics boorishly insisted that I would never walk onto a stage when I could leap. The truth was slightly less exaggerated, although I admit I sometimes did have certain sets rearranged to facilitate a more affecting entrance. After all, such was part of the drama. But this particular drama, I sighed to myself as I studied the gaudy decorations, was quite unlike any other. Any additional exploit would pale by comparison.

I turned to go, feeling the pangs of hunger myself, and started to walk off the stage. A motion in the wings suddenly caught my attention, and I swiftly froze.

It was Prudy.

She stood near the gas box, the wooden framework that housed the wheels and levers that controlled the theater lighting, and she bumped into it sharply as she hurriedly tried to back away. She was as beautiful as ever, despite a frumpy maid's costume that detracted from her exquisite form, but her face was a mask of stark horror. She turned to run, and I tried to follow, but something seemed to literally hold my boots to the polished wooden floor.

"Prudy! Please, wait!"

She stopped, hesitantly, turning slowly back to face me, but her green eyes refused to yield their animal fear. Or their hatred.

I held one hand out towards her, struggling to find the

proper words. Yet for once in my miserable life I was absolutely speechless. "I'm sorry, Prudy," I finally managed to croak. "I don't know what I could say to you that could ever make amends, but as God is my witness, I am sorry."

"You hurt me, Johnny," she whispered, so softly I could barely hear. "I loved you so much, and all you could do was hurt me."

I wanted to melt through the damned stage. "I know. God forgive me, I just don't know what came over me. So much has happened, Prudy, so many terrible things. I didn't mean to make you the brunt of my anger. I know it's not possible, but if you could ever find it within yourself to forgive me, I would be forever in your debt."

Slowly, guardedly, Prudy stepped out of the wings and started towards me. The gas footlights, turned up for the rehearsal, flickered across her face, and I saw the jeweled tears. For a single moment, as she drew ever closer, I was certain she was about to strike me. I even braced myself, never more deserving of any chastisement. But then, as she stopped less than three feet away, the look on her face turned from rage, to confusion, to unabashed yearning, and she suddenly threw herself into my puzzled but grateful arms.

"Oh God, Johnny," she sobbed into my shoulder. "I missed you so much! You have no idea how much I missed you!"

"Nor I you," I told her honestly. "Please forgive me, Prudy. I'm so damnably sorry."

"I do, Johnny! I do forgive you!" She drew back, staring up at me with a look that spoke of such incredible adoration that I nearly fell apart. "Just don't leave me again! Please, promise me you won't leave!"

I had to turn away. "Christ, Prudy, don't say that. You have no idea what you're asking. You don't even know who I am."

"Yes I do," she cried, clutching at my arm. "I know who you are, Johnny Booth. I know what you are, what your reputation is like. Do you think mine is any better? All I want is someone who will love me, that's all." She pulled herself against me, and I felt her soft body quaking with sobs. "I just want you to love me, Johnny."

I stumbled away in genuine anguish. "Prudy, please, don't do this! Don't force me into this situation, I beg you!"

She gaped up at me. "Situation? You mean love? Don't force you to love me, is that it?"

"No, no, that's not what I mean! Damn it, Prudy, you just don't understand. I can't be with you. I can't be with anyone." I waved a hand at the props and scenery that cluttered the stage. "This world, this life, it's over for me, Prudy. Forever."

She shook her blonde head in bewilderment. "Johnny, you're not making sense. You're a great actor, and you're still so young! Your career, our careers, are still ahead of us!" She fairly gushed with her enthusiasm. "We can play the stage together, Johnny, all over the world! Just you and I!"

"No, God damn it!" I whirled around and sent a prop chair clattering with an angry kick. Prudy backed away, frightened, and I struggled to suppress my temper. I righted the chair, which had lost a slat, and leaned against it until my breathing, and my rage, had sufficiently calmed. "Prudy, please, listen to me, just for a moment. Do you know why I haven't been on the stage for so long?" I tapped at my throat when she warily shook her head. "Because I'm losing my stage voice, that's why. It's very nearly gone. I've been telling everyone it's bronchitis, but I can't lie, not anymore. The doctors tell me that if I continue acting, then it won't be long before I can barely speak above a whisper."

"But how, Johnny? Why?"

I sighed in disgust. "Because I'm me, Prudy. I'm John Wilkes Booth, prima donna of the stage! Everything the wretched critics have ever said about me is true. My arrogance, my conceit, all of it. I've never been an actor; I've been my father's son, my brother's brother. I leaped onto the stage with nothing more than my name to guide me."

I looked away from her, frowning towards a sea of vacant chairs that began to blur before my eyes. "My father was a drunk and a madman, Prudy, but he was the best goddamn actor the world has ever known. He managed to teach Junius and Edwin, in those last lucid years before he died, but I was too young to have his guidance. My brothers stepped out with the proper training, but not me." I shook my head in bitter chagrin. "Not that it would have mattered. Hell, I was too damned headstrong to let anyone tell me anything. Edwin tried to warn me, of course. 'Projection, dear Wilkes'," I feigned in my brother's deep baritone. "'It's all in projection!' But I shouted, Prudy, like the rankest of amateurs, which is exactly what I've been ever since. Whatever success I've enjoyed has been nothing but a goddamn fluke! And now . . ." I looked back at her, trying unsuccessfully to choke back my tears. "Now it's all over. All of it."

Prudy shook her head emphatically. "But, surely there's a chance, Johnny! With proper rest, and maybe a better doctor—"

"No, Prudy. There's no chance at all. Besides . . ." I turned to flash a sullen glare at that damnable box. "There are other issues that are just as . . . devastating."

There was a sudden noise, from the front of the theater, and I realized the cast was returning. I pulled myself erect, smiling wistfully at a young woman who would never know that the love she carried for this pathetic fool burned just as deeply for her within my own heart.

"I have to go, Prudy. I'll be leaving Washington soon, and for good, I'm afraid. I hope . . . pray . . . that you can try to remember me with some little affection. Though after tonight I seriously doubt that will be possible."

"Why would that be so, Johnny?" She was shaking now, so

wretched were her sobs, and her lovely face was shining with bitter tears. "I could never think of you with anything but love! You know that!"

I suddenly found it impossible to meet her eyes. "Goodbye, Prudy." I reached out quickly and took her in my arms, kissing soft, salty lips, then gently pushed her aside and hurried out of the theater.

My last glimpse of her was as she stood alone, in the middle of the stage, looking as lost and hopeless and forlorn as I myself felt.

Chapter Thirteen

If it were done, when 'tis done, then 'twere well
It were done quickly.

~~~Macbeth~~~

It was time.

I closed my watch, quaffed what remained of my precious brandy, then sealed the envelope and tucked it into my coat pocket. I had written and rewritten the letter several times, since my earlier efforts that afternoon, burning the wasted attempts in the little Franklin stove in the corner. Now, at exactly nine p.m., the words were as eloquent and enlightening and as devastating as I could possibly make them, and they would have to suffice.

I opened the desk drawer and scrabbled through a pile of love letters and playbills, until my fingers brushed the cold metal of the object I sought. It was a second pistol, not much larger than Prudy's, which I had purchased some weeks before as part of our kidnap plans. I primed the tiny muzzle loader with a brass percussion cap, then slipped it into my left pocket. I had no idea as to whether I would need it, since Stanton had sworn that Grant would not be present. But the bastard had already provided me with far too many surprises since this wretched affair began, and damned if I was taking further chances. I picked up the dagger, as well, and slid the steel blade into the side of my riding boot. Then I stood up, tugged my hat over thickly pomaded curls, and went out to kill the president.

My horse was waiting for me at Pumphrey's, the stable just behind the National. Normally I would have rented the mount from Howard's, where I had sent Louis Wiechmann for his surrey, but Jim Pumphrey had mentioned to me that he had recently obtained a fleet mare, a bad little bitch, as he put it, and I wanted the fastest animal I could find. Pumphrey was true to his word. The mare was black as midnight, and as fast as a cat. I took the reins from the Negro stableboy and tried her out immediately, exhilarating in the rush of the balmy night wind and the ring of her steel shoes on the cobblestones. She had me in the alley behind Ford's in the wink of an evil eye.

It was known as Baptist alley, owing to the former church, I presumed, but there was nothing at all that was holy about it. The stench from the refuse boxes and outhouses was a fetid as in any other, and the horse even tried to shy away as I dismounted. I had the devil's own time holding on to her while I pounded at the backstage door.

It was several minutes before the heavy door swung open, and I recognized Ned Spangler's glaring face in the sudden spill of gaslight.

"Damn it to hell," he whispered sharply. "Stop your goddamn bangin'! Don't you know there's a play goin' on in . . . John Wilkes? What the hell are you doin' out here?"

"I need to come inside for a few minutes, Neddy. Think you could hold my horse for a bit?"

He frowned at me in puzzlement, then shook his gray head. "I'm needed inside, John Wilkes. They're havin' some trouble with the scenery. Wait a minute, an' I'll go fetch Peanut."

Ned bobbed back inside, and I waited in the malodorous starlight while the horse tried to yank my arm from its socket.

The door opened again, and Peanut stumbled out, calmly munching on a candied apple. "How do, Mr. Booth?" he said with his crooked grin.

"I need you to look after my horse, Peanut," I said as I handed him the reins. "I have to tell you, though, she's a bad one. Think you can keep her still?"

The boy took the leather straps with a casual nod, then promptly shoved the apple into the mare's mouth. Instantly, the animal quieted, calmly swishing its tail as it savored the peculiar treat.

Peanut smiled up at me. "Reckon she'll be still enough, Mr. Booth."

I shook my head in genuine awe, tossing the boy a silver dollar as I went inside.

Backstage was bustling with activity, as was usual during any performance. Actors and stagehands rushed to and fro, fumbling with ill-fitting costumes and bulky props. I saw Harry Hawk standing in the wings, leaning on his cane as he awaited his cue. From his lackadaisical grin, I gathered he must have been able to achieve his desired level of sobriety. Another actor, a young bit-player named John Matthews, stood nearby. I tiptoed up behind Matthews and tapped him on the shoulder.

"Wilkes!" he whispered as he spun around. "Good to see you! Harry said you came by today, but I must have missed you."

"Matt," I said quietly. I pointed towards the brightly glaring stage. "How goes it, tonight?"

He shrugged thinly. "Same as ever. I'll be glad when this damned play is gone, and I can move on to better roles."

I nodded sympathetically, though I had little hope for Matthews' acting future. His thinning hair and weak features mandated a career of character pieces, which was exactly what he was playing now. I tugged at his oversize suit coat. "Who do they have you playing, anyways?"

"I'm Coyle, the Trenchard's attorney." He drew himself up, smugly. "Veddy, veddy British, you know."

I chuckled, then glanced past him, where Laura Keene and the dowager actress, Harriet Muzzy, who played a stuffy English matron, were bemoaning the news that their proper British society was about to be sullied by the arrival of a backwoods American relative. I followed the inane dialogue for a brief moment, surprised to see how warmly it was being received by what appeared to be a full house, though the bright footlights made it difficult to see anything but wavering silhouettes beyond the stage. The same was true of the presidential box, yet I thought I caught a glimpse of three or four shadowed figures within the twin windows. I tapped Matthews again.

"Big crowd?"

He nodded. "For Good Friday, it certainly is. Though I'll wager they're all here to see the President."

He's here, then?"

"Oh, yes," Matt said eagerly. "The play even stopped when he arrived, and the orchestra played 'Hail to the Chief'. Everyone stood up and cheered." He pointed to the distant box. "He's up yonder, see?"

"Indeed. Listen, Matt, could you do me a favor?"

"Certainly, Wilkes. Anything for a fellow thespian."

I tugged the envelope from my pocket. "I'm leaving for a short trip, and I need to have this delivered to the *National Intelligencer*."

He frowned at the sealed packet. "The newspaper?"

"Yes. I would drop it by myself, but I'm leaving tonight. Think you could take it round for me?"

Matt took the envelope warily. "I suppose so, but . . . isn't that a Secesh paper, Wilkes?"

"What difference does it make? The war's over. Please, Matt, I need to make sure it's delivered directly to the editor, Mr. Seaton. Can I trust you to see to it yourself?"

Matthews nodded, extending his hand. "You may rely on your old friend!" He stuffed the envelope into his pocket, as a gruff voice suddenly whispered from the prompter's box.

"Mr. Matthews, your cue!"

Matt threw me a plucky shrug. "Sorry, Wilkes. Have to go."

He started towards the stage, but staggered suddenly backwards as I reached out and yanked at his collar. "What the hell? Wilkes, I've got to go on!"

I tugged him towards me, pressing my face desperately close to his. "Matt, for God's sake, you've got to promise me you'll deliver that packet! A number of lives depend on it!" I shook him roughly. "Do you swear to it?"

Matthews searched my face with frightened, befuddled eyes, but nodded fervently. "Of course, Wilkes, of course! I swear to it! The package will be delivered!"

"Mr. Matthews, please! You're on!"

I let go of him, nodding slowly. "Don't fail me, Matt. Please."

He straightened his coat, tugged at his floppy tie, then turned and headed once more for the stage, flashing me a final anxious scowl over one rumpled shoulder. "Ah, my dear Trenchards," he called nervously to the waiting actors. "A house full of company, I see . . ."

I watched as the play swiftly resumed, then turned and made my way backstage, behind the heavy curtains, towards the narrow corridor that led to the actor's entrance out front.

There was a door halfway along the hall, dimly lit by wall sconces, which led directly from Ford's into Taltuval's Star Saloon. A convenient niche, which I'd often employed quite eagerly. Just as I did now.

Taltuval's was even less praiseworthy than Volkner's; merely a narrow bar and a scattering of rickety stools. Most of them were full, but I found an empty spot and tossed a few coins at the owner.

"Whiskey," I told Peter Taltuval. "And leave the bottle."

"Whiskey?" The skinny German pulled a bottle from a mirrored shelf, then slid it in front of me with a puzzled grin. "Not your usual poison, Mr. Booth."

"Not a normal night, Peter. Not by a damn sight." I took a

heavy gulp, reeling from the searing bite, but instantly felt my nerves begin to calm.

Taltuval set a worn deck of playing cards on the battered bar. "Some of the boys been playin' Monte tonight, Mr. Booth." He flashed me a gap-toothed smile. "Care to try your luck?"

I shook my head. "There's hardly a chance of that, Peter. As Shakespeare said, I am fortune's fool." I reached out and turned over the top card, solely out of curiosity, then smiled ruefully at the grinning joker. I held it up for Taltuval. "You see?"

Tossing the card aside, I opened my watch and set it next to the whiskey bottle. Nine fifty-two. Eight more minutes, and the entire wretched plan would unfold. Abraham Lincoln would be dead, and John Wilkes Booth would be immortal. And infamous.

Eight more God-damned minutes.

God, but my mind was spinning. As much as I hated Lincoln, as much as I truly believed him responsible for all the ills the South had suffered, I wanted no part of Stanton's murderous ambitions. It would be one thing to strike a blow for the Cause, but whose cause this death truly serving? Whose fate was genuinely at stake? If I were to do this, it would be for the South; for Atlanta, and Vicksburg, and the thousands upon thousands of good men who had died, simply because they believed in the right of a state to choose for itself.

Yet there was still a chance to leave this madness behind. I pondered the possibility as I took another drink. I could still try to run. It was conceivable that I could make it to a safe haven long before Stanton's cronies could track me. There were numerous Confederate allies, and not just in Canada. Even now, according to the papers, pockets of Rebel resistance still fought on valiantly despite Lee's surrender. There was even talk of a plan to move the Richmond government, now in desperate flight, to Mexico or South America. The Cause could yet survive, and I could play an intrinsic part. All I needed was a fast horse, which was waiting for me behind Ford's. Oh, yes, I could easily get away. And once Matthews delivered my package to the Intelligencer, the entire world would know the truth of Stanton's treachery.

And in any event, John Surratt had been right; not even a cold-hearted bastard like Stanton would be barbarous enough to hang a woman.

Let slip the dogs of war, I smiled grimly to myself, for all the good it might do them. John Wilkes Booth would be no Union lackey. I was going to run.

I finished the whiskey, slid the bottle away, and snatched up my watch.

"Care for another, Mr. Booth?"

"No thanks, Peter. I'm afraid I haven't got the time."

I started towards the door I had entered, the one that led to the actor's corridor, but found that a burly patron had chosen that spot for a drunken sprawl. I muttered a curse and headed instead for the front entrance.

Tenth Street was nearly deserted, and I paid scant attention to those few souls who traipsed the cobblestones. My mind was fixed instead on the stage door, less than fifteen feet from Taltuval's, and the spirited nag that waited in the alley. Fifteen feet to blessed freedom.

A match suddenly flared across the street. A brief glimmer, to be certain, but enough to catch my attention. I turned a cursory glance to see a figure leaning in a doorway, half-hidden in the shadows, but the glow from his cigar was enough to illumine the broad shoulders and ponderous frame.

And even in the dark, I knew Luther Baker was grinning.

I came to a dead halt, literally quaking with helpless rage. Baker lifted the cigar, in a mocking wave, and to me the tiny red glow was like a demon's eye. I watched it waver in the sultry night, never in my life having felt more despondent.

It seemed an eternity before I could finally manage a few halting steps, and then only backwards. When I did, I unwittingly stumbled into a tall man who was loitering outside the theater. I shied away from him, quickly mumbling a terse apology.

"Sorry, friend, I didn't see you there."

"That's quite all right," a deep voice rumbled affably. "Just enjoying a breath of fresh air. What with all the cigar smoke inside, one could easily suffocate before the third act."

"Indeed." I forced a swift smile and started past him, but was suddenly stopped by a firm, yet oddly gentle, grip on my arm.

"Pardon me, friend," the man's voice grew pointedly curious. "Aren't you young Booth, the actor?"

"What? Booth?" I was several moments recovering from my anxious start, as well as the sight of that bastard across the street. "Yes," I finally managed to croak. "I am John Booth."

The man nodded, and I perceived a thin smile in the flickering lamplight. He was an odd-looking fellow, wearing a rumpled gray suit and an exceedingly wide-brimmed hat. He appeared to be middle-aged, perhaps older, with a curly, graying beard, and had it not been for his cultured tones, I would have thought him a backwater rube.

"I thought as much." His grin widened, as he bent down to peer at me from beneath the peculiar headgear. "You resemble your late father. He was a mesmerizing performer! Absolutely mesmerizing!"

I nodded curtly, trying to pull away, but that big hand held me fast. I frowned up into the bearded face. "If you don't mind, I am late for an appointment, Mr.?"

"Whitman. My name is Walt Whitman. I have seen you perform, as well, young Booth. You have talent," he said earnestly, ". . . but you lack your father's flair, his sense of passion. I mean no offense, of course, but I seriously doubt you'll ever achieve his stature."

I jerked away from his grasp, seething, but just as quickly felt the anger slip away. I straightened my clothing and nodded wearily. "Perhaps, Mr. Whitman, what you say is true. My father was indeed a man of rare abilities." I glanced across the street, where Baker continued his laconic slouch. "But believe me, sir, when I leave the stage for good, I will undoubtedly be the most famous man in America. Good evening to you, Mr. Whitman."

I swiftly brushed past him and hurried into Ford's.

Chapter Fourteen

If th' assassination
Could trammel up the consequence, and catch
With his surcease, success; that but this blow
Might be the be-all and the end-all here.
       ~~~Macbeth~~~

"Evenin', Mr. Booth."

Ford's doorman, John Buckingham—Old Buck, as most of us knew him—grinned his toothless grin from his ticketer's booth just inside the lobby entrance. He worked his wrinkled gums around a wad of tobacco and eyed me curiously, nodding towards the curtained doorways that led to the auditorium. "Play's nearly over, you know."

"I've seen it before, Buck," I replied with a smile of my own. "Just looking for . . . an acquaintance. Mind if I pop in and have a look around?"

"Why, surely," he laughed. "Never need a ticket from you, Mr. Booth." He watched me as I started for the closest door. "Is she pretty?"

"Who?"

"Your acquaintance." He threw me a sly wink from between the gilded bars. "The one you're lookin' for?"

I returned the mischievous smirk. "They're all pretty, Buck."

I stepped through the curtain as the old man dissolved in a lecherous cackle.

The auditorium smelled of perfume and pomade and popcorn and sweat; a heady mix that wafted above neatly groomed heads on a fog of cigar smoke. As Mr. Whitman had said. it was very nearly overpowering. I stood in the back, behind the endless rows of silk gowns and dapper suits, and watched as the curtain slowly rose to reveal Laura Keene, Harry Hawk, and Harriet Muzzy together on stage. The pivotal act, for the play and my life, had begun.

Turn away.

I found myself wishing to God I had accepted Taltuval's offer of a second bottle. My hands were shaking uncontrollably, nearly as rapid as my breathing, and my coat was streaked from sweat that had started to stream like rivers.

Turn away!

The voice seemed to hiss at me through the smoky darkness, above the applause and insipid laughter. *Turn around*, it whispered sharply. *Just turn around and walk away. Past Old Buck, through the stage door, and out to that demon horse. Turn around and run like holy hell . . .*

Right into the muzzle of Luther Baker's gun.

I drew in my breath, wiped my palms against my coat, then turned and hurried up the carpeted stairs to the dress circle.

The balcony was just as crowded as the lower mezzanine, though its patrons were decidedly less elegant than those in the more expensive seats below. Yet they were all concentrating on the play, and no one noticed my rapid stride towards the presidential box.

Laura Keene was bewailing her character's lack of a true love. "All I crave is affection," she sighed to Harry Hawk.

"Do you now," he queried sadly. "I wish I could make sure of that, for I've been cruelly disappointed in that particular."

Harriet Muzzy picked up her skirts and swept in towards him, and for her size, such a sweep was duly impressive. "Yes, but we are old friends, Mr. Trenchard, and you needn't be afraid of us."

I stepped up to the outer door of the box. Just outside, hard against the plaster wall, sat an empty chair. A bodyguard's chair. I nudged the rickety furnishing quietly aside, then slowly gripped the doorknob and pulled it open. There was no challenging cry, no shout of alarm; only the rippling, giddy chortles of the enraptured crowd.

On stage, the actors had erupted into a scathing argument, as the American cousin suddenly revealed he wasn't what he claimed to be. I kept one ear to the dialogue as I slipped inside the box and closed the first door behind me.

"Not heir to the fortune, Mr. Trenchard?" Harriet Muzzy demanded.

"Oh, no," Harry admitted. "Nary a red cent."

It took a few moments for my eyes to adjust to the sudden, total darkness. I was in a narrow hallway, barely large enough to turn around in, facing two more doors which led directly to the presidential seats. Once I could see well enough, I suddenly noticed a short length of scrap wood, left behind by Neddy and Peanut, no doubt, propped in a corner. I quickly snatched it up and jammed it tightly between the wall and the main door, then quietly turned to the closest door.

Someone had drilled a small hole, just above the knob, undoubtedly a previous bodyguard who had found an ingenious way of observing his charges without disturbing their entertainment. I utilized the peephole myself, crouching down to blink inside. There were four persons within; two women and two men, and it took only the briefest instant to recognize President Lincoln. Old Abe sat to the extreme left, in Harry Ford's big rocking chair, smiling languidly down at the stage below. A small but plump woman sat to his right, apparently Mrs. Lincoln, since the President gently cradled one of her hands in his own. The other couple, on the opposite side of the box, shared a narrow settee, and I started briefly at the sight of a blue uniform on the man. Yet I saw no gun, or saber, and he seemed far more interested in the lovely young woman who sat next to him than he did in the President. I stood up, reaching into my pocket to grasp Prudy's derringer, and opened the door as slowly, and as silently, as was possible.

Turn away.

Harry Hawk was now extolling his fervent but penniless love to Laura Keene. "You crave affection, you do. Now, I've no fortune, but I'm boiling over with affections, which I'm ready to pour out all over you like applesass."

I stepped inside the box, quickly lifting the pistol towards the back of Lincoln's bearded head.

Turn away.

Laura Keene flounced off stage, aghast at the thought of marrying a destitute American, while Harriet Muzzy made another of her massive swoops towards poor Harry.

"I am aware, Mr. Trenchard, that you are not used to the manners good society, and that alone will excuse the impertinence of which you are guilty!"

Turn away!

It took all of my will to thumb back the tiny hammer. There must have been an audible click, lost to my pounding ears, for I saw the girl sitting next to the army officer suddenly glance up towards me. Her lovely mouth made a stark, silent O.

"Don't know the manners of polite society, eh?" Harry Hawk drew himself up with a grand sneer, shaking his cane at the expansive backside that was haughtily exiting the stage. "Well, I guess I know enough to turn you inside out, old gal . . . you sockdologizing old man-trap!"

My trembling finger curled tightly around the trigger, as the entire audience, and President Lincoln, roared out with unbridled laughter. That's when the girl finally found a voice to her horror. Her scream, and the crack of the little gun, came almost as one.

The next few seconds were a hellish blur. I saw Lincoln slump forward, as his wife added her own horrific screams to the girl's. The army officer jumped to his feet, leaping towards me with a look of murderous outrage. I stumbled backwards, shoving the still-smoking derringer into my right coat pocket, while desperately groping for the second gun in my left. I had barely managed to level it at his glaring face when he swung at me and sent the pistol flying. He was nearly on top of me, both hands scrabbling for my throat, when I remembered the knife in my boot. I reeled aside, drew the dagger, and slashed at his flailing arm. There was a spray of blood, and he fell back, howling in pain and fury. Frantic, I turned and lunged for the flag-draped box.

The theater had gone deathly silent. I was dimly aware of hundreds of gaping faces, including Harry Hawk's, as I vaulted over the box and jumped for the stage. Something suddenly yanked at my leg, and I realized with a desperate start that my spur had caught in the God-damned flags. I landed squarely on my left foot, hard, and heard the sickening snap above my ankle. Yet oddly enough, I felt no pain; only the maddening, exhilarating tremor of shock that coursed through my veins like fire. I had done it. Before God, man, and the entire unthinking world.

I had murdered Abraham Lincoln.

I staggered to my feet, still unaware of any real pain, and swiftly hobbled towards the wings. It seemed to take an eternity, as I rushed by an incredulous Harry Hawk, then plowed through a knot of gawking, slack-jawed actors which included Laura Keene, Billy Ferguson, and, much to my grievous dismay, dear Prudy. I met her baleful gaze only briefly.

"I'm sorry," I choked as I stumbled past her. "I'm so sorry."

Old Neddy was near the back door, and I saw him glance down at the bloody knife I was still brandishing. He lurched out of the way in alarm, just as I grabbed the latch, and that's when the entire theater seemed to shake off its petrified stupor.

"Stop that man!"

"He's shot the President!"

"My God, he's killed Mr. Lincoln!"

Their frenzied cries followed me out as I threw my weight against the door and staggered out into Baptist Alley. Peanut was sitting on a packing crate, crooning a tuneless song to that devil's horse, and I yanked the reins from his startled hands and inadvertently sent him sprawling. I pulled myself into the saddle, just as three or four men came charging through the door, and barely managed to escape their lunging grasp with a spur to the mare's black flanks. She bolted down the alley with a hideous scream.

The cries of alarm swiftly faded behind me, and the night became an endless rush of wind and flickering lights. I galloped headlong through Washington City, so damnably fast I had no idea which direction I was headed. I was aware of nothing, save the hammer of hoofbeats, which rivaled the pound of blood within my ears. I turned the horse this way and that, oblivious to the passages I chose, sending unwary pedestrians and back-alley drunks scurrying for desperate cover. Only after a breathless dash, when the mare was fairly heaving beneath me, did I finally slow her breakneck pace and bother to take my bearings.

The huge dome of the Capitol was darkly silhouetted against the night sky. I was on Maryland Avenue, according to a street sign beneath a flickering lamppost, and headed due east. A fortuitous circumstance, much to my relief, and I turned the gasping horse and trotted, far more slowly this time, towards the south. There were no obstacles to my path, no streets filled with soldiers in bloodthirsty pursuit. Even Luther Baker was nowhere in sight within the shuttered doorways and darkened alleys. In a matter of anxious minutes, I had left the city behind and was in sight of the Navy Yard Bridge.

The bridge was a narrow causeway that spanned the Anacostia River, a tributary of the broad Potomac, between Washington and the Maryland peninsula. The army guarded the rickety wooden structure, as it did all of the roadways in or out of the capital, and I saw several dark figures, all with arms, loitering about the entrance to the span as I slowly rode up. My leg had finally begun to hurt by now, wretchedly, and I fought to keep my face relaxed as a surly-looking sergeant stepped towards me and held up a hissing lantern.

"Halt," he called laconically. "Who are you sir, and where are you going?"

"My name is Boyd," I said with a curt shrug. "I'm heading for Bryantown, across the river." I leaned forward, studying his stubbled face in the flickering light. "By way of the T.B. Road."

He showed no reaction at that; merely took in my dusty suit and the horse's lathered flanks. "Seem to be in one godawful hurry, friend," he frowned at length. "Have you any papers?"

Slowly, the panic began to creep in, as I realized that Stanton's promise had been another contemptible lie. I held my composure, keenly aware that I was no longer armed, save for the knife which I had returned to my boot. I swallowed the bile in my throat, then once more tried the password. "Perhaps you didn't hear me," I said evenly. "I'm traveling by way of the T.B. Road."

"Sergeant Cobb," a different voice suddenly called, "let the man pass." A young officer, whose face I could not discern, stepped out of the shadows and stood just beyond the halo of wavering light from the lantern. He pointed towards the bridge. "I said let the man pass, sergeant. He's free to go."

The sergeant shrugged, lowering the lantern as he waved me on. "Ride on, friend."

I cast a silent salute towards the officer, but he only turned and walked away, back towards a small guard shack near the side of the road. Frowning curiously, I spurred the horse with my good leg, then cantered across the murky waters and rode, with a trembling sigh of relief, into Maryland.

Chapter Fifteen

Things without all remedy
Should be without regard;
What's done, is done.
       ~~~Macbeth~~~

It was nearly midnight before I finally saw any sign of the others.

Lloyd's Tavern, at the southern edge of Surrattsville, was closed and shuttered for the night. I wanted a brandy, or any liquor, as the pain in my leg grew damnably worse by the minute. Yet I could not bring myself to rouse anyone from slumber for fear of drawing suspicion. Despite the password's success, and the fact that there had been no bodyguard at Ford's, I still could not bring myself to trust that bastard Stanton. The very ease by which the night's bloody events had transpired was the thorn that pricked at my soul. Something was not quite right, but damned if I could fathom what it might have been.

I watched the road, in the cloudy starlight above Lloyd's, from a copse of magnolia trees. The mare was tired, and losing a shoe, judging by the way she'd been limping shortly before I'd halted, and I was fearful as to whether she could go much farther. If George ever showed up, I reasoned he could tend to her, since he was nearly as adept at smithing as he was at drinking. If George ever showed up.

If anyone ever showed up.

I suddenly heard a distant clopping, and peered through the leaves as a lone horseman crested a small rise and rode quickly towards Lloyd's. It was too dark to be certain, but I thought it might have been Davey. I watched as he reined the horse to a wary halt, then saw him glance anxiously, eagerly about in the darkness.

"Mr. Booth," that familiar youthful voice called nervously. "Are you there, sir?"

"I'm here, Davey." Slowly, I nudged the mare from cover and started towards him. "Where's Lewis?"

Davey shook his head frantically. "Oh, Mr. Booth, it was terrible! Just terrible! Lewis went inside Mr. Seward's house, just like you told him. He had a tonic I brought along, and they let him in right quick."

I winced, both at the pain in my leg, and his anguished face. "What happened?"

"I don't know, Mr. Booth. I waited outside, like you said, an' all of a sudden, I heard godawful noises from inside. Men an' women both, Mr. Booth, shoutin' like the very devil was after 'em!"

I remembered the look in Paine's dull eyes. "Maybe he was. Did Lewis ever come out?"

Davey nodded. "Yes, sir, finally. He come runnin' out the front door, wavin' a knife over his head an' shoutin' 'I'm mad! I'm mad!' I think he might have killed some people, Mr Booth. A nigger servant came runnin' out after him, yellin' about a murder."

I looked away in disgust. "Christ!"

"Last I seen him," Davey continued bleakly, "he was runnin' down the street with that nigger an' a bunch of other folks right behind him. I didn't feel much like tryin' to catch up with him, so I rode on out here." He stared at me forlornly. "I hope you ain't mad, Mr. Booth."

"At you?" I shook my head quickly. "No, Davey, you did right in leaving the bastard. God knows what happened to him." I glanced back towards the road. "Or to George, for that matter." I groaned sharply, as the mare's sudden prance jarred my swollen leg.

Davey peered at me anxiously. "You all right, Mr. Booth?"

"I broke my leg in Ford's. I think I'll have to find a doctor before too long." I gestured towards the darkened shadow of the tavern, handing him a thick wad of currency. "Do me a favor, Davey. Go and wake up old John. Tell him you want a bottle of brandy and a couple of guns. Pay him as much as he wants, but for God's sake, don't tell him I'm out here."

Davey nodded obediently, then tugged at his horse and started off. He stopped, suddenly, glancing back at me in the darkness. "Did you do it, Mr. Booth? Did you kill Mr. Lincoln?"

"Yes, Davey. I killed him."

The boy said nothing, but it was several long moments before he finally turned away.

I waited at the side of the road, watching as he disappeared around the back of the big tavern. Moments later, a lamp flickered to life in an upper window, and the pale light wavered brightly as it was carried down through the house. Several tense minutes passed, as the throb in my leg grew more and more intolerable. The mare had recovered enough of her strength to grow skittish, and every dancing move was sheer agony. I would have shot the bitch dead had I but had a gun.

I saw Davey ride around from the tavern, carrying a bulky canvas sack in one hand. He reached inside and pulled out a bottle, grinning broadly as he rode up to me.

"I got three bottles, Mr. Booth. And a pair of Colt's pistols. Mr. Lloyd wasn't too happy about gettin' up, but he smiled considerable when he saw the money. He wanted it all, though."

I took the bottle eagerly. "The hell with the money." The first long, grateful pull went down in a single gulp, and I instantly felt better. Davey handed me one of the pistols, which I shoved into my belt. "We'd best be going, Davey boy. We've got a long ride ahead of us."

"Where we goin', Mr. Booth? John lit off for Canada, so

how we goin' to find his hideout?"

"We're not. We'll make our way back across the Potomac, then head south, to New Orleans."

"New Orleans?" Davey pointed north, over his shoulder. "I don't understand. I thought you said your money was in Canada?"

"My money was in Canada," I smiled. "But it didn't stay there. Jacob Thompson sees to it that my Montreal accounts only stay active for a few days. After that, he transfers all my funds to the Merchant's Bank of New Orleans." I reined the mare towards the road. "I never intended to go north, Davey. I just wanted certain people to think I was."

He nodded, slowly, falling in beside me. "What about George, Mr. Booth? Shouldn't we wait for him?"

I shrugged. "He knows the way to Port Tobacco. Besides, the idiot probably went and got himself drunk. The hell with him and Lewis both." My leg was still in agony, despite the brandy, as we struck out towards the west. "I've got to find a doctor, Davey. My leg is killing me."

"There's a sawbones lives nearby," Davey offered. "Fellow John said was a friend. Name of Mudd, I believe."

I knew the name. "Do you know where he lives?"

"Sure do." The boy took the lead, at a gratefully gentle pace, and we traversed the next few miles in weary but tranquil silence.

We found the doctor's farmhouse near the edge of what Davey called Zekiah Swamp. It was an evil-looking place, especially in the dead of night, and I was thankful when we turned our horses away from the mist-enshrouded bog.

Davey and I reined up in front of the darkened house. Somewhere in the back a dog began to bark; a large dog, by the vicious sound. I prayed he was tied to a stout leash, as Davey slipped off his horse and reached up to help me down from the mare. Yet dismounting was no facile affair, and between my cry of pain and that hound's incessant snarl, lights were soon burning within the farmhouse.

"Who's out there?" An angry male voice roared from an upper window. "Goddamn it, I've got a gun! Who are you?"

"Is this Dr. Mudd's house?" Davey called anxiously. "There's a man down here hurt bad, sir! We need your help!"

I heard the window slam shut, and it was only moments later that a light appeared at the front door. A tall figure, clad in a flowing nightshirt, stepped out on the rambling porch. He held up a kerosene lantern, as Davey slipped an arm about my shoulder and helped me limp across the lawn.

"What happened to him?" the man queried. I saw a pistol clutched tightly in his other hand, which he kept lowered, yet ready. "Has he been shot?"

"Broke his leg," Davey said. The boy looked up at me anxiously, as we reached the narrow steps. "Easy now, Mr. Boo—"

"Boyd," I said quickly. I looked up at the man. "My name is Boyd. Like the boy said, I've broken my leg. Damned horse decided to take a tumble on me. Are you Dr. Mudd?"

"I'm Mudd." He set the lantern, and the gun, on the porch banister, then hurried down the steps to take my other shoulder. "Let's get you on inside and take a look."

The two of them had to virtually carry me up the steps, no easy feet since I was a good deal taller than both. A woman waited in the doorway, a plumpish farm wife, wearing a heavy robe and an anxious, sleepy frown.

"Fetch my bag, Frances," Mudd called to her as we negotiated the last step. "Then go wake Cyrus. This fellow needs my attention."

The woman disappeared with a nod, and the three of us managed to sidle through the front door and into Mudd's small but comfortable parlor.

Mudd nodded to a narrow settee. "Let's put you down here."

The pain, when Mudd lifted my leg to the sofa, was unbearable, and I nearly tore away twin handfuls of velvet upholstery.

"Your leg's swollen pretty bad, Mr. Boyd. I'll have to cut off this boot."

I managed a thin smile. "Long as you don't take the leg with it."

He chuckled at that, then motioned for Davey to turn up a nearby lamp.

I finally got a good look at him in the bright light. Sam Mudd was a gangly man in his mid-thirties, with a thick goatee and rapidly receding blond hair. I knew him only vaguely, having met him once at a Copperhead rally in Baltimore shortly before the war began. I found myself praying, as he glanced from my leg to my face, that his own memory was equally poor.

"You say your horse threw you?"

"Fell on me, to be honest. I think the bitch had tired and decided to ride me for a change."

Mudd took in my expensive riding clothes. "You're out awfully late, Mr. Boyd. This country isn't safe, especially if you don't know the roads."

I nodded wearily, glancing at Davey. "So I've discovered. Think you can set the leg, doctor?"

"I think so, though you'll want to stay off of it for awhile."

Mudd's wife came back into the room, carrying a small leather satchel. I glanced past her and suddenly started. Hovering obsequiously in the doorway was a squat but powerfully-built Negro.

"Thank you, Frances," Mudd smiled as he took the bag. He looked at me, and apparently caught my wary frown, for he nodded over his shoulder towards the black. "My farmhand, Cyrus. He'll have to hold you down while I set that leg, Mr. Boyd."

I forced a sullen nod. "If you say so."

Mudd rummaged through the bag. "Frances, why don't you fix some coffee for these gentlemen?"

I eyed him keenly. "No offense, doctor, but haven't you got anything stronger?"

Mudd laughed. "Fetch Mr. Boyd that bottle of medicinal brandy, Frances."

The woman echoed her husband's chortle. "Certainly, Sam." She smiled at Davey. "What about you, Mr . . ?"

I saw Davey's sudden, anguished look of confusion.

"Tyson," I said suddenly. "This is my companion, Mr. Daniel Tyson."

"Yes, ma'am," Davey sighed, flashing me a grateful smile. "Dan Tyson, that's me. Some coffee'd taste real good about now."

"Fine," Mrs. Mudd smiled. "Why don't you come along and give me a hand? I'm sure your friend will be fine in my husband's hands."

I nodded for him to go, and Davey followed the woman out of the parlor, sidling past the sullen, silent Negro. The black leaned against the doorway and eyed me curiously.

"Damn," Mudd suddenly scowled over his open bag. "I can't find my shears to cut that boot."

"Here." I pulled the dagger from the opposite boot. "Use this."

Mudd took the weapon, guardedly, casting me a puzzled glance. He studied me intently. "Do I know you, Mr. Boyd?"

"No," I said flatly. "You do not know me, Dr. Mudd." I held his pensive stare. "You do not know me."

For several long moments, he frowned at me over the knife. Then he quickly shrugged and began to cut away the thigh-length boot. He eased the ruined leather off my throbbing leg and tossed it aside. "Cyrus," he called to the Negro. "Go find me something to make a splint. Bust up one of those apple crates out back and bring me the slats."

The black nodded briefly as he left. "Yes, suh."

"Your slave?" I asked Mudd.

"I've never owned any slaves," the doctor said quickly. "Cyrus used to be a slave further south, down in South Carolina, but he's been free for two or three years, now. Besides, slavery was the one issue I never was able to justify, despite my love for the South. I assume you are a Southerner, Mr. Boyd?"

"I am. I take it you believe Lincoln was right in freeing the niggers?"

Mudd tore open my trouser leg. "I don't hold any great esteem for Mr. Lincoln. But I don't believe any man belongs in bondage."

I drew in my breath. "What if someone were to kill Lincoln, Dr. Mudd? How would you feel about that?"

He thought for a moment, then shook his head bleakly. "I think, Mr. Boyd, that it would be another useless death on top of thousands more."

"So you would have no sympathy for his assassin?"

He slipped a pillow beneath my swollen calf. "To what end? His action would not have accomplished a damnable thing, for either North or South." He looked up at me pointedly. "Would it?"

I leaned my head back against the sofa and made no reply.

Davey and Mrs. Mudd came back into the room. The woman held a cluttered tray, while Davey was gleefully munching on what appeared to be biscuits slabbed with thick ham. He gave me one of the sandwiches, which I devoured ravenously.

"Here you are, Mr. Boyd." Mrs. Mudd handed me a bottle of cheap brandy, which smelled heavily of peaches. "Sam only prescribes this in limited quantities," she said with a glib smile. "Isn't that right, Sam?"

"I think in Mr. Boyd's case we can increase the dosage."

Mudd nodded at me gravely. "Drink as much as you can, Mr. Boyd. This is going to hurt."

I had drained the entire bottle by the time the Negro, Cyrus, had returned with twin handfuls of wooden slats. Mudd waved him to my side.

"Take him by the shoulders, Cyrus. Hold him fast, now."

I readied myself, flinching only slightly when the black's big hands slipped firmly over my shoulders. Mudd handed me a folded wad of linen bandages, then took a stance at the end of the settee and gently gripped my leg. "I want you to put that cloth between your teeth, Mr. Boyd, and at the count of three, bit down as hard as you can. Ready? One. Two. Three!"

He jerked the leg sharply. I heard the crack of bone, felt a stab of unbelievable pain, then slipped away into a sudden and welcome darkness.

Chapter Sixteen

To fly the boar before the boar pursues,
Were to incense the boar to follow us,
And make pursuit where he did mean no chase.
~~~Richard III~~~

I awoke to the magnificent aroma of bacon and coffee. I was still stretched out on Mudd's sofa, my leg encased in a makeshift but adequate splint, but the pain had gratefully subsided to little more than a dull throb. I sat up, tossing off the heavy quilt that Mrs. Mudd had apparently draped around me, and glanced blinkingly around.

"Good morning, Mr. Boyd." Dr. Mudd was sitting in a nearby chair. "I trust you slept well. That sofa isn't the most comfortable bed, but I thought it best to let you stay where you were."

I gave him a sleepy grin. "I feel remarkably refreshed, Dr. Mudd. Doubtless that will even improve, once I've tasted the source of that glorious scent."

Mudd laughed as he stood up. "Frances' cooking is famous for its recuperative effects." He walked to the window and opened the drapes to an incredibly bright spring morning. "Just let me have a look at that leg, first."

The doctor returned to crouch next to the sofa. "Good. Swelling's gone down considerably. I think after a few day's rest—"

"No," I said quickly, struggling to rise to my good leg. "I can't stay any longer, I'm afraid. I have business in Washington that won't wait."

Mudd shook his head reprovingly. "But you've got to stay off that leg, Mr. Boyd. The slightest jar could cause it to set poorly. You could end up crippled for life."

"I promise, doctor, that I shall rest as soon as it's humanly possible. In the meantime, I have to be on my way. Where is my friend, Mr . . . ." I froze in sudden horror, realizing that I had forgotten Davey's alias.

"Tyson?" Mudd offered. He eyed me with an increasingly wary scowl. "He's in the kitchen, having breakfast. Why don't you at least do the same? You can't travel on an empty stomach."

I nodded swiftly. "Yes, yes, of course. I appreciate all your kindness, Dr. Mudd."

"Not at all, Mr. Boyd," he said with a shrug, but the caution never left his blue eyes. He reached down to help me up. "This way."

The Mudd's kitchen was a spacious affair, warm and sunny, and filled with even more of the enticing smells. Davey sat at a large oak table, his youthful face jubilantly smeared with the remnants of a mammoth breakfast. He grinned through butter and syrup as Mudd and I hobbled in, waving to a nearby chair.

"Mornin', Mr. Boyd! Have some of these flapjacks an' molasses!"

Mudd carefully eased me into the chair, and I nodded hungrily at Davey. "I believe I shall have a portion of everything, Dan. It looks wonderful."

Davey handed me a platter of steaming biscuits. "Mrs. Mudd cooks better'n my own ma." He glanced around furtively. "'Course, I can't ever let ma hear that."

Mrs. Mudd, who was stirring a pot on the huge cast-iron stove, laughed delightedly. "Why, thank you, Mr. Tyson. I promise you, your secret is safe with me."

I started to help myself to an assortment of the incredible fare, when Mudd suddenly glanced out the kitchen window. "Rider coming," he said, more to himself than the rest of us. "Looks like Jake Simmons, the postal rider from Bryantown.

Wonder what he's doing out here this early?" The doctor pulled his hat from a peg on the wall, then started out the back door. "I'll be back in a minute, Frances."

I looked over at Davey, who shared my anxious dread. I nodded briefly towards the door. "We'd best be going, Dan."

"But you haven't touched your breakfast, Mr. Boyd." Mrs. Mudd hurried over to the table. "Surely you don't mean to let Mr. Tyson enjoy it for you?"

"I'm afraid it can't be helped, good lady," I smiled as I labored to get up. "Our business keeps us constantly on the move. Tomorrow it may be Mr. Tyson who starves."

She frowned at me sharply. "Well, then, at least let me pack a few things for you, to eat along your journey."

Before I could object, Mudd came back into the house. His face was stark, ashen, and I felt my hand inch instinctively towards my hidden Colt.

"Why, Sam!" Mrs. Mudd exclaimed. "What is it? You look like you just saw a ghost!"

"That was the postman from Bryantown," the doctor said flatly. His eyes never left mine as he spoke. "He said John Wilkes Booth, the actor, shot President Lincoln last night in Ford's Theater. He's not expected to live."

"Dear God!" Mrs. Mudd threw flour-covered hands to her face.

"Booth got away," Mudd continued. "Apparently headed south. Jake says the army is out in droves."

I suddenly felt my heart begin to race.

Mudd's wife was nearly in tears. "My God, Sam, why would he kill the President? The war is over! Oh, God, but this is terrible!"

I forced my eyes away from Mudd's livid glower, fumbling in my pockets with a shaking hand. "Here is payment for your help, Dr. Mudd." I set a small stack of gold coins next to a platter of bacon. "Again, thank you for your hospitality."

The doctor said nothing, but merely continued to fix me with that piercing, angry glare.

I nodded at Davey, and he hurriedly stepped around the table to take my shoulder. The two of us quickly left the kitchen, as fast as my one-legged hobble would permit, and hurried through the house to the front entrance.

The Negro, Cyrus, was currying our horses near the Mudd's stable. I waved at him sharply as Davey and I approached. "You, nigger! Saddle those goddamn horses and be quick about it!"

The black glanced at me silently, then swiftly and obediently began to saddle both mounts. He stepped aside, holding out the reins to my mare.

"Want me to he'p you up in the saddle, suh?"

"Mr. Tyson can assist me," I snarled. "I don't need your help."

He nodded quietly and walked away.

It was arduous, struggling into that saddle, but I was agile and Davey was strong, and for once that damned mare cooperated. Davey had swung up into his own horse, and the two of us were starting to turn away, when Cyrus suddenly appeared again. He held out a pair of oblong objects in my direction.

"Reckon you could use these, suh? I made 'em this mornin'."

It took me a few seconds to realize what he held in his ebony fist were crutches, hewn from sapling boughs and cushioned with heavy rags.

I frowned from the crutches to his dark, impassive face. "Did Mudd tell you to make those?"

The black shook his head slowly. "No, suh. Done made 'em myself. Way you was hurtin' last night, I reckoned you might have need of 'em."

"You reckoned?" I shook my head in genuine confusion.

"You don't even know me, nigger. Why would you make me crutches?"

Cyrus shrugged his broad shoulders. "I knowed you was hurtin', suh. Reckon that's all I needed to know." He pressed the saplings, still sticky with sap, into my hands. "Hope they's long enough." He flashed me a brief, obsequious smile, then turned and quickly walked away to his morning chores.

I sat there, dumbfounded, as the mare began an impatient dance.

I knowed you was hurtin'.

It was several moments before I could bring myself to tie the crutches to the saddle.

Davey and I were halfway down the narrow path to the road when I heard the farmhouse door suddenly bang open behind us.

"Booth! Wait!"

I stiffened at the sound of my name, once more reaching for the gun. Dr. Mudd ran up between our horses, breathing heavily as he grabbed at the mare's reins.

"Why, Mr. Booth?" His pleading look was intolerable. "Why?"

I shook my head swiftly, struggling to keep my face composed. "My name is Boyd, Dr. Mudd, and I have no idea what you're talking about."

He refused to let go. "Damn you, sir! I have no sympathy! Do you understand me? I won't turn you in, you can rest assured of that much. But I have absolutely no sympathy for you whatsoever!"

I stared down at him blankly. "For that, doctor, you have no need to trouble yourself." I yanked the reins from his angry grasp. "I have none, either."

Davey and I struck out again, leaving Mudd alone in the dusty road.

Davey glanced back anxiously. "He knew who you were,

Mr. Booth."

"I heard, Davey."

The boy was silent for a moment. "He said Mr. Lincoln weren't dead."

"I heard that, too."

We rode in pensive silence, for a long, long while.

Davey chose the western fork of the T.B. Road, one that he said led to the Potomac a few miles ahead. The day was magnificent, filled with chirping birds and glorious sunshine. A sharp contrast to the previous day's gloom. But I felt no elation at nature's beauty. I pondered instead the doctor's parting words, as well as his report of soldiers. And every so often, as my good leg tapped against the dangling crutches, I thought of Cyrus.

I knowed you was hurtin'.

I shook my head in bitter perplexity. Nothing at all made sense anymore. Absolutely nothing.

There was a small creek up ahead, one of the Potomac's myriad tributaries, and Davey spoke of a ferry that plied the deep waters.

"We'll have to ride across," the boy shrugged. "Ain't no way to ford it this time of year."

I nodded absently, still musing over the week's incredulous events, as we started towards the ferry landing. It was truly nothing more than a flatboat, tied to a rickety wharf at the edge of the gray water. The place was thick with bulrushes, and a small, tumble-down shack stood near the dock. But there didn't seem to be any sign of activity on or near the ferry. No sign of life whatsoever. There was something else that seemed out of place, some tiny vexing annoyance, and we were nearly upon the sagging dock when I finally realized what it was.

The birds had stopped their jubilant singing.

I pulled up the horse, sharply, and hissed for Davey to do

the same. He turned to frown at me.

"What's wrong, Mr. Booth? We're nearly there."

I shook my head, slowly reaching for the Colt. "Davey, there's no one about. No ferryman, no one."

"Maybe it's too early," the boy shrugged. "Reckon we might have to—"

"Davey, run!" I screamed the warning just as the first blue forage cap popped up in the window of the shack, followed by the blue-steel barrel of a Spencer carbine. "It's a goddamn trap!"

Three rifles had cracked from the thick reeds before we could whirl our horses and start a reckless dash through the trees. A bullet plucked at my sleeve, so I turned to loose a frantic shot behind me. I nearly fell from the saddle at what I saw. Yankee soldiers were spilling like maddened ants from the edge of the riverbank, dozens of them, and I realized that Edwin Stanton had never intended to keep his wretched bargain.

Davey and I rode like men possessed, whipping the horses into a lather before we had run the first mile. I had no idea of where we were going, or how far; the only thought to which my desperate mind could cling was survival. Behind us, the soldiers had retrieved their own horses, and the dust of their pursuit seemed to loom closer with every fearful glance behind. My leg had begun to throb again, despite the heavy splint, bouncing as it was against the mare's heaving flanks. Yet the animal herself showed no impediment, not even the broken shoe—could it have been Cyrus again? She had settled into a fleet, confident stride that swiftly outdistanced Davey's poor gelding, as well as the charging cavalry.

I passed the Mudd farmhouse, rounding a small bend in the road, and I had to pull the horse up sharply to take the curve. There in the middle of the road, where the forest threatened to claim the narrow track, a lone, blue-coated horseman sat astride a huge mount and blocked my way. I yanked the mare to a screaming, rearing halt, and saw with gut-wrenching horror that the rider was calmly smiling along the length of his leveled revolver.

"End of the line, Reb," Luther Baker called out gamely. "Throw down your gun."

I fought to bring the frenzied mare under control, never once turning my furious glare from the gun's black muzzle. "Kill me now, you son of a bitch! I don't intend to give Mr. Stanton the pleasure of seeing me hang!"

Luther's grin slowly widened. "Makes me no never mind. I get my money either way." I saw his thumb draw back the hammer.

The shot rang out, and I flinched, bracing myself for the sledgehammer blow and the searing, white-hot pain.

Neither ever came.

When I opened my eyes, Luther was on the ground, howling in fury as he struggled to pull himself from beneath his dying horse.

Davey suddenly rode up beside me, waving his smoking pistol. "Come on, Mr. Booth! They'll be on us any second!"

"You go on, Davey." I waved him on, nudging the mare forward, and cocked my own pistol as I grimly eyed the struggling Yankee. "I have business to finish."

Davey turned a frantic scowl behind us, where a churning cyclone of dust roared ever closer. "Please, Mr. Booth!"

But I ignored the boy, calmly walking the horse towards Luther Baker.

Luther had abandoned his attempts to free his pinioned leg, and was stretching a desperate hand towards his fallen Colt. His scrabbling fingers fell scant inches short, and he looked up when the mare's hoof nearly crushed them. He fell back in bleak resignation. "Go on. Reb," he said flatly. "You know you've been wantin' to!"

I aimed the gun between his malevolent eyes.

"Mr. Booth!"

I lifted the gun, glaring down at him. "Go on back," I hissed through clenched teeth. "Go on back and tell that devil you work for that I did exactly as he asked! You hear me, Baker? Exactly as he asked!" I pulled the mare away, sidling around his dead horse. "Come on, Davey! I'm right behind you!"

Davey spurred his horse, once we cleared the obstacle, and the animal leaped the low rail fence that bordered the road. The boy was headed straight towards the dismal hell of Zekiah swamp. I hesitated, for the briefest of moments, glancing back at an incredulous Luther Baker. Something told me to go ahead and put a bullet through his filthy brain, and it was all I could do to restrain myself. I loosed a shout of frustrated rage, then spurred the mare and vaulted over the fence.

The soldiers had reached their fallen comrade by then, and a dozen or so shots followed after us, buzzing through the dogwood trees like angry hornets. But then all was quiet. By the time I caught up with Davey, near a wide, foul-smelling stand of black water, there was no sign of pursuit.

The boy's perennial grin had returned. "They won't be comin' after us, Mr. Booth. Ain't nobody fool enough to travel through this swamp, not 'less they know the way."

I glanced nervously over my shoulder. "I should imagine they'll find someone who does."

"Don't make no difference," Davey shrugged. "Won't be nothin' for 'em to follow. Come on."

With Davey leading the way, we turned the horses and plunged into the cold, stagnant water, and slowly began a nightmarish trek through that malevolent swamp.

Chapter Seventeen

I have set my life upon a cast,
And I will stand the hazard of the die.
                    ~~~Richard III~~~

"After being hunted like a dog through swamps, woods, and last night being chased by gunboats, I am here in despair; wet, cold, and starving, and with every man's hand against me."

I put down the pencil and rubbed at my aching eyes. The light from the little candle was barely enough to see my own hand, let alone the pages of the daybook, but I had to finish the entry. Despite the chill that shook my body, despite the fever that alternately ebbed and soared, I was determined to set the entire affair to some sort of permanent record. It was all that was left me.

I glanced around, in the sputtering glow that wavered within the little tobacco shed. The place reeked, and more than once I heard the rustling of vermin within the darkened corners, but such dismal conditions were barely a shrugging concern by now. The past twelve days had turned Davey and me into animals; nearly as wretched as the runaway slaves who had doubtlessly been trailed through the same filthy swamps. And for the first time in my life, I felt a twinge of regret for those pathetic creatures. As well as for my own miserable existence.

Twelve days. An eternity, so it seemed, slogging from sunup to damnable sunup through that devil's mire. Davey's cheerful optimism, that no man would dare follow us through Zekiah's hell, had proven woefully premature. Stanton was obviously not about to let me slip away, and the winding trails were thick with bluecoats; so numerous that it actually seemed they outnumbered the very mosquitoes. The boy and I had been forced to travel only by night, and on foot, since we had killed both horses out of fear that their terrified neighing might give us away. It nearly broke my heart when I slit the mare's throat, after only the second day of running, but the jangle of spurs and sabers through the tangled beech trees was a decidedly sobering balm. Cyrus' crutches were nearly useless in the watery muck, and my leg screamed in agony with every step. And to make matters worse, both Davey and I began to shiver and burn with the first signs of malaria. Yet we managed, somehow, to elude our pursuers, even to the point of finally crossing the Potomac on a misty night, in a stolen rowboat, and under the very nose of a Federal gunboat. We were now in Virginia, somewhere near Port Royal or Fredericksburg, though as to exactly where I wasn't truly certain. But in simple truth, I did not care. We were still alive.

There was a sudden rustling from outside the barn. I snuffed the candle, tossing aside my leather-bound diary in exchange for my revolver. I bit back the sudden, searing pain in my leg, which seemed to grow worse with every staggering mile, and leveled the gun through the darkness. Someone was approaching the shed.

The narrow door slowly creaked open, and a dark head bobbed in with the spilling starlight.

"Mr. Booth?"

I lowered the gun, sighing. "Come on in, Davey."

The boy pushed open the door as I relighted the tiny candle. He held up his canvas sack. "Got us some hardtack and bully beef, Mr. Booth. And the newspapers, just like you asked."

I took the folded papers eagerly. "Did you have any trouble getting the issues I wanted?"

Davey shook his head, dropping to his bed of tobacco leaves and attacking a tin of beef with his dagger. "No sir, nary a bit. Fellow at the store had all of 'em. Said he was thinkin' of paperin' his wall, since they'd carried such good news." He looked up with an anxious smile. "Reckon he didn't like Mr. Lincoln."

I nodded absently, fervently scanning the tabloids. They were all copies of the *National Intelligencer*, dating back to the fifteenth. As Davey ravenously devoured his first full meal in days, I read through the baleful headlines.

Lincoln was dead. He had died the following morning, according to the paper, roughly about the time Davey and I were leaving Dr. Mudd's. There was no mention of an attack on Vice-President Johnson—not that I seriously thought George might have actually made the attempt—but there was a tremendously disturbing account of a murderous assault on Secretary Seward. It was expected that the Secretary of State would live, despite the grievous knife wounds he'd suffered, as would the three others, two relatives and a servant, whom the mad assailant had also slashed. I shook my head in revulsion.

George Atzerodt and Lewis Paine were both in custody, according to the latest editions, and a massive search was on for John Surratt. The suspects, the paper reported, were being held incommunicado, at the War Department's request. I felt a baleful chill, remembering Stanton's ominous words from that night in the hotel, and I seriously doubted if George and Lewis would ever see the light of day again. The article continued, with a terse report, that several others had also been arrested, each with possible ties to the assassin, and included one Ned Spangler, Dr. Samuel Mudd, and a Mrs. Mary Surratt . . . .

"Jesus Christ," I heard myself rasp. The paper began to tremble within my clenched fists. Stanton had done it. The filthy son of a bitch had actually gone and done it. "Jesus Almighty Christ."

My own name was scattered across every wretched page, though each entry carried a malignant adjective like fiend, demon, and monster. I shrugged off the revilements, thumbing quickly through the next few issues, yet the only news that continued to scream from the bold-type print, all the way though the twentieth of April, was the fact that the diabolical slayer of our beloved president was still at large. Matthews had failed me. Or, more likely, Edwin Stanton had somehow performed his devil's magic and intercepted him. And in either event, my last hope for exoneration was gone.

I threw the papers aside with an angry curse.

Davey glanced up from his third can of stringy beef. "What's wrong, Mr. Booth?"

"Everything, Davey," I sighed dismally. "As flies to wanton boys are we to the gods. They kill us for their sport."

He offered a puzzled smile. "Reckon that's theater talk?"

"Shakespeare," I nodded. "It means we're cursed, every goddamn one of us. God, but my leg hurts! I'll probably have to have it set again once we get to New Orleans." I waved a tired hand towards the food. "Open me a can of that beef, will y—"

"You there! In the barn!"

The voice made Davey and I both scrabble frantically for our weapons. Once more I blew out the candle, and we waited fearfully in the darkness as a pair of footsteps swiftly trudged up to the door.

"Hey, there," the voice called again. "Are you fellows awake? It's me, Garrett!"

Richard Garrett was the old man who owned the barn, as well as the little farm it sat on. He had reluctantly agreed to shelter Davey and me for the night, apparently satisfied with our claim to be Confederate soldiers making our way home. He shuffled up to the door and tugged it open, blinking rheumy eyes at the sudden flare of my match.

"Sorry to bust in on you boys," the old man shrugged, "but I need you to make room for another feller. One of your own, in fact."

Davey and I glanced wearily at one another as Garrett stepped aside. A second man, clad in a tattered Rebel uniform, walked into the shed.

"This here's Sergeant Ruddy," Garrett explained.

"Rhodie," the soldier corrected. He smiled a bleak greeting at both of us. "Tom Rhodie. Fourth Virginia regiment, though I'm really from Maryland."

"John Boyd," I offered gamely, swiftly slipping the pistol aside. "This here's Dan Tyson. We were with the Richmond Grays."

Old Garrett swept disdainful eyes over my mud-spattered suit. "Funny you boys ain't wearin' no uniforms."

"Lots of us didn't have no uniforms," Davey retorted quickly. "Didn't mean we couldn't fight."

Sgt. Rhodie, a malnourished scarecrow with a shock of copper-red hair, seemed unaffected by our lack of military dress. His hungry gaze was fixed instead on the cans of beef. "You fellows wouldn't have some of that grub to spare, would you?"

"We would," I nodded. "And welcome."

Garrett watched briefly as Davey opened a couple of cans for the starving Reb, then turned his grizzled scowl to me. "Reckon you boys should be comfortable enough in here. I'd let you sleep up at the house, but the missus ain't partial to strangers. 'Specially with the Yanks lookin' for them fellers who killed Abe Lincoln."

"We'll be fine," I told him, forcing my voice to maintain a casual air. "You reckon they'll catch 'em?"

He shrugged. "More'n likely. 'Specially since they's offerin' a hunnerd thousand dollar reward."

Davey and I shared a sudden, doleful gape. Stanton was taking absolutely no chances whatsoever.

"That's a lot of money," I mused grudgingly. I held the

old man's guarded stare. "Money like that could set a man for life."

"It could," Garrett nodded. His lips pursed tightly. "But only if he was partial to Abe Lincoln. And to blood money." He turned to leave, reaching out to close the door. "You fellers get a good night's sleep. But I want all of you gone, come mornin'."

Sgt. Rhodie finished his beef and started to gnaw on a piece of hardtack. "Reckon I wasn't too fond of Old Abe," he mumbled around the cracker. "But damned if I can see the sense in killin' him."

I took the last can of beef from Davey and picked at the contents. "To be honest with you, friend," I told him after an anxious while, "I'm not all that certain that I can, either."

Rhodie finished his food and languidly stretched out in a corner of the shed. Davey gathered up the empty tins, shoving them into the dirty sack, then quietly dropped to his knees and began to pray. I watched him for a moment, then took up my diary, which was actually a daybook from the year before, and continued to pencil in my dispirited thoughts.

"God cannot pardon me if I have done wrong, and it's with Him to damn or bless me. And for this brave boy with me, who often prays—yes, before and since—with a true and sincere heart, was it crime in him to serve me? If so, why can he pray the same? The little, the very little, I left behind to clear my name, the government will not allow to be printed. And so ends all . . ."

I felt my bowels suddenly begin to churn. That damnable swamp had taken its toll within and without, so I tucked my diary into my coat pocket and snatched up the Negro's implausible crutches. The saplings had started to crack in several places, and the cushioning had long since fallen away, but I could not bring myself to make new ones. That black's kindness, so damnably innocuous, had somehow touched a nerve. I was beginning to believe I had been wrong, about so many things in my wasted life, but like everything else in this interminable nightmare, I could not find any sense in it. Yet neither could I part with Cyrus' crutches.

Davey looked up from his prayers. "Where you goin', Mr. Booth?"

"To answer nature, Davey boy." I struggled painfully to my good leg. "Best to take care of it outside, since this shed already smells bad enough. Hand me one of those newspapers, will you?"

The boy complied, and I hobbled out into the sultry night.

There was a dense clump of juniper, a good fifty or so feet from the shed, and I hobbled inside and clumsily got my trousers undone just in time. It was an awkward affair, what with my leg stretched out before me, but one that I was fast becoming used to. I waited until the last wrenching spasm had finally subsided, then put a page of that newspaper to good use and started to button up. That's when I heard the low, unmistakable rumble of galloping horses.

I stayed crouched there in the bushes, watching as a dozen or so dark horseman rode in through the trees and reined up in front of Garrett's big house, some hundred yards away. There were sudden, angry shouts, then lamplight flickered through the windows, and I saw a lone figure step out through the front door. Two mounted men rode closer to the long porch, and there were more shouts, and the figure, whom I reasoned to be old Garrett himself, suddenly pointed in my direction. The horsemen turned their animals and charged towards the little shed.

"Oh, Christ," I whispered, reaching under my coat for a Colt that I realized I had left behind. "Davey . . ."

The soldiers, for that's what their clanging sabers and unslung carbines revealed them to be, rode up to the shed and swiftly dismounted. In an instant, several torches had been lighted, and the barn was surrounded by the flickering light.

"Booth!" A tall, bearded officer slipped off his horse and stepped cautiously towards the door. "Come on out of there, you miserable bastard!"

I recognized the voice, as well as the massive outline, and drew further back in the shadows, wishing to God I had pulled the trigger back there on the T.B. Road.

"Come on out, Booth," Luther Baker shouted again. He drew his pistol. "I know you're in there!"

"Mr. Booth ain't in here!" Davey's voice was a panicked screech. "He ain't in here, whoever you are!"

Luther cocked his big head to one side. "That you, Herold? Don't play with me, boy! I ain't partial to anyone who shoots my horse! You want to see your mama an' sisters again, you'd best come on out! An' bring that bastard Booth along with you!"

"Mr. Booth ain't in here!" The misery in the boy's voice was heart-rending. "I swear it, mister!"

Luther turned to his men and motioned with the gun. "Fire the barn!"

Several torches arced towards the rickety shed, which was instantly set ablaze.

"Come on out," Luther roared, backing away from the licking flames. "'Less you want to burn to death!"

The door swung open, and Davey rushed out, both hands waving frantically above his head. "Don't shoot! Please, don't shoot!"

Three troopers rushed forward and seized the boy, dragging him roughly away from the barn. Luther and several others leveled their guns at the blazing shed. A second figure, coughing and sputtering, was suddenly silhouetted in the crackling flames.

The gun in Luther's hand spat a single yellow tongue.

"Go fetch him," the giant growled laconically, nodding towards the now-empty doorway.

Two soldiers rushed inside, then just as quickly emerged, dragging a limp, smoldering form between them. They threw the body to the ground, just as the shed collapsed in a brilliant geyser of flame and sparks. One of them kicked at Rhodie's body.

"Looks like you got him, lieutenant."

Davey started to struggle with his captors. "That ain't Mr. Booth!"

Luther wheeled to face him. "Look, boy, it don't do no good to try an' help him now. You worry about your own goddamn neck!"

"But it ain't Mr. Booth!" Davey shook his head swiftly, and in the falling flames I could see the anguished tears on his youthful face. "That feller's name is Rh—"

Luther suddenly swung the pistol, smashing the barrel hard against Davey's face. I watched in helpless fury as the boy crumpled to the ground and lay still.

"Tie an' gag that piece of shit," Luther barked. "We got what we came for. Let's get movin'."

"Lieutenant Baker," A stocky sergeant suddenly called from his crouch near Rhodie's body. "I think you should take a look at this . . ."

Luther stalked over to the man, scowling. "What is it, Congers?"

The soldier pointed to the corpse with a frown of his own. "I think that boy may have been telling the truth. This man isn't Booth."

"What?" Luther grabbed a torch from another soldier's hand, then crouched down to peer at the smoke-blackened face. "What the hell are you talkin' about?"

"I've seen Booth on stage, lieutenant," the sergeant insisted. "He has black hair. This man's hair is red."

"He's an actor," Luther snapped. "He could have dyed it." Yet I could see, by the flickering torchlight, the look of confusion that twisted his bearded face.

Sgt. Congers shook his head adamantly. "No, sir. This man is not John Wilkes Booth. I'd stake my life on it." He stood up, waving to the soldiers who were trussing poor Davey. "You men! Fetch some water and revive that man! We've got to find out—"

"Congers," Luther called sharply, "let it go."

The sergeant turned around, frowning. "Sir?"

"I said let it go." Luther lumbered to his feet, nudging the body with the toe of his boot. "We got our man."

"But lieutenant—"

Luther suddenly reached out and seized the startled trooper by the front of his blue blouse. "God damn it, Congers, I said we got our man!" He pulled the sergeant's face close against his own. "I don't particularly fancy another twelve days of ridin', do you? Besides," he added with his malevolent sneer, "that corpse is worth a hundred thousand dollars."

Congers pulled himself away from the giant's grasp. "But how the hell do you intend to prove it's Booth?" He jabbed an angry finger towards the unconscious Davey. "That man knows he's not! And so will anyone else who sees the face!"

"That man," Luther said flatly, nodding at Davey, "will keep his mouth shut, if he wants to keep his family alive an' safe. So will every man here." He turned to glare at the rest of the assembled soldiers. "Ain't that right?"

One by one, I saw each man nod anxiously in the fading firelight.

Luther turned back to Congers. "An' as far as that corpse is concerned . . ." He cocked his revolver once again, bending down to press the muzzle against poor Rhodie's lifeless face. I blanched in sickening horror when he pulled the trigger.

"Now then," Luther sighed as he straightened up. "Let's get this mess back to Washington."

The soldiers lifted poor Davey, and the unfortunate Sgt.

Rhodie, across a pair of horses, then the entire troop swiftly mounted and rumbled away.

All except for Luther Baker.

The giant stood quietly, as the vapid chirp of crickets slowly replaced the fire's hiss, and glanced around in the darkness. And then, as I watched in indescribable horror, he began a swift, deliberate stride towards the juniper.

"Come on out, Reb," he called with his perpetual sneer. "You don't want me comin' in after you."

Slowly, despairingly, I pulled myself erect with the crutches. Without question, my life was over, and it made precious little sense to delay the inevitable. My wasted life, once so famed and admired; gone for absolutely nothing. Yet I had no time to repent, no courage to plead, and no will to ponder as to how any man could have given himself over to such lunatic schemes of grandeur. Sweet Jesus, I had not even the strength left to cry.

Luther drew in closer, stepping through the brush. "Never really thought you'd get away, Booth," he smiled as he swung up the pistol. I heard the ominous click of the hammer. "Did you?"

I forced my eyes to meet his, summoning a final, desperate bravado. "Go to hell, you worthless son of a whore!"

Luther's grin suddenly widened, as he inexplicably lowered the hammer and drew back the Colt. The last thing I heard, just before the barrel smashed against my face, was the bastard's sadistic laughter.

Chapter Eighteen

There is a tide in the affairs of men
Which, taken at the flood, leads on to fortune;
And we must take the current when it serves,
Or lose our ventures.

~~~Julius Caesar~~~

Somewhere a ship's bell rang three times; a doleful sound in the humid darkness. I lay on the wet straw and listened to the muted tones, pensively wondering as to whether the hour they tolled was day or night. I had lost all track of time, shackled and hooded as I was, but, wonder of all incredulous wonders, I was still very much alive.

I was deep in the hold of a ship. I could tell by the incessant, nauseating roll and the slap of water against a wooden hull. I reasoned as to how it might have been a warship, even an ironclad, since the pounding of leather boots on metal decking echoed almost constantly from somewhere above, along with an endless drone of shouted orders and clanging steel. I was alone, of that much I was certain, lying in a fetid cell on a pallet that was far more lice than straw, and with only rats for company. They skittered across my bad leg and poked about at my clothing, but as yet none had been inclined to bite. As a consequence, I tried to lie as motionless as possible; a feat that was hardly difficult considering the incredible pain in my leg.

How long I had been there I did not know. Perhaps a day, perhaps longer. I had awakened from Luther's Colt-induced slumber with a blinding headache, and then to the panicked realization that I was, indeed, quite blind. And paralyzed. But my fears had subsided significantly when I discovered that my head was merely encased in a hood of filthy canvas, while my hands were manacled tightly behind my back. My legs were free, undoubtedly because of the fracture, which throbbed now even worse than my head, but a heavy iron chain shackled about my midsection made any thought of escape completely pointless. Not that I even had the slightest bit of strength left to try.

Now and again, footsteps would sound from somewhere close by, but only twice since I'd regained consciousness did I hear the click of the bolt being drawn back from my cell door. On both those occasions, a silent, solitary entity entered the room and pulled me quickly, but not without genuine caution, to my good leg, then guided me across the tiny cell, where my hands were freed long enough to allow me to relieve myself into a reeking bucket. Afterwards, the same gentle hands lowered me back to the straw and offered a canteen of brackish water through a slit in the canvas hood. I had whispered fervent thanks to my unseen Samaritan, and tried to evoke some little information as to my whereabouts. But he had held his baleful silence, snapping the manacles fast about my chafed wrists once again before leaving me alone with the vermin.

A million dismal thoughts, each one significantly worse than the other, began a frantic parade through my aching head. For whatever fathomless reason, that demon had chosen not to pull the trigger. What, then, was actually to be my fate? What end did Edwin Stanton have planned for his hired assassin? Obviously there could be no trial. Far too much had already transpired to make certain his diabolical conspiracy remained cloaked. Upon what stage would John Wilkes Booth take his final bow? A midnight gallows? Perhaps even a yardarm, and on this very ship? Or would Stanton merely have me wrapped in more canvas and chains, then dropped over the side in the dead of night? The possibilities were as endless as they were terrifying. It even occurred to me, and with no small amount of growing dread, that I might simply be left to rot, here in this squalid hull, until the rats finally grew brazen enough to bare their razor-sharp teeth . . .

The footsteps sounded once again outside the cell door.

I tried to sit up, scaring away several of my rodent cellmates as I heard the steel door clang open. There was more than one guard, this time; I heard the scrape of multiple soles on the slimy floor.

"Get him on his feet," a far too-familiar voice suddenly growled.

Two pairs of hands heaved me upwards, ignoring my leg. I cried out at the searing agony.

"Careful there," a second voice said, and not unkindly. "His leg is broken."

"The hell with his leg," Luther Baker snapped. "He yells again an' I'll cut it off!" I felt a fist grab savagely at my coat lapel. "You hear that, Reb? You want to stay alive, you keep quiet! Strike his irons off, Morrison."

I heard the rattle of keys, and the manacles suddenly dropped from my hands, followed by the heavy chain around my waist. I rubbed at my swollen wrists, hoping against hope that the hood would follow, and risked a tentative, rasping query. "Where . . . where are you taking me?"

A heavy hand slapped against my already splitting skull. "That hood must have made you deaf! I told you to shut up! Now get him topside, an' be quick about it!"

The guards quickly hauled me through the door and down a narrow corridor, so tight that all three of us were forced to maneuver sideways. I kept a desperate silence the entire distance, biting my tongue against the stab of white-hot pain each time my foot scraped the metal flooring. I was lifted along a steep stairway, hauled down another corridor, and then, finally, I was manhandled bodily up through a narrow hatch. The rank confines of that wretched hold suddenly gave way to the familiar tang of the Potomac, and I drew in a blessed gulp of cool air, totally oblivious to the stink of rotting fish and foul scuppers. The brisk chill and the absence of light through that miserable hood told me it was night, and I started to shiver violently in my damp clothing. But in all honesty, I cared very little. I was finally, mercifully free of that hellhole.

"Down the plank," I heard Luther bark.

My captors carried me down a rickety gangplank. I could hear the water lapping and gurgling below. Then the pace became more plodding, and the footing beneath more solid, and I knew we were somewhere on shore. The ground beneath my skidding feet turned from mud to gravel to broken flagstones, and, after a short while, I heard the rusty squeak of a heavy door.

"Inside," Luther ordered. The door banged shut behind us, and then we were swiftly winding our way down a flight of concrete steps.

"Far enough," Luther finally said. "Leave him right here."

The guards set me down, suddenly, but before I could tumble to the ground, some sort of brace was shoved in under my right arm, and I leaned on it quickly, heavily. I heard the receding scrape of boots on the steps, and for several long seconds, thought myself to be completely abandoned. Then the hood was forcibly yanked from my head.

I was in a long, low room, the first thing I noticed when my eyes finally ceased their interminable blinking. The floor was bare earth and the ceiling was moldering brick, and the only light came from a small lantern that hissed and flickered near a mound of freshly turned dirt. Then I looked closer and saw that the dirt had been scraped from a shallow trench in the floor, and when I peered into the trench, my heart very nearly stood still. The lantern light was dim, but not so much that I couldn't recognize the oblong object that lay stretched within the length of the ditch.

It was the canvas-shrouded form of a corpse.

I glanced around, forcing back the bile in my throat, and caught sight of Luther Baker. He hovered nearby with his massive arms folded across his chest, and, for once, an oddly dispassionate scowl on his face. It was all I could do to force another wary question.

"Where am I?"

"You're in the basement of the Arsenal Penitentiary, Mr. Booth." The voice came from the stone staircase, as a short, dark, pudgy figure slowly waddled out of the shadows and into the dancing light. Edwin Stanton offered a curt little nod as he stepped closer. "A pleasure to see you once again."

"Jesus." I collapsed against the brace, which I suddenly realized was one of Cyrus' makeshift crutches. "Sweet merciful Jesus."

Stanton was carrying a small satchel in one hand, which he swiftly opened, reaching in to withdraw a tiny, gleaming object. He held it up, and I recognized Prudy's derringer. "Is this it, Mr. Booth?" His dark eyes gleamed with genuine curiosity. "Is this the gun with which you killed him? I thought at first it was the one we found in the theater, until Lieutenant Baker informed me that that one was still loaded."

I held his gaze in glowering contempt and made no reply.

"Remarkable," he said at pensive length. "Truly remarkable. You are a most impressive individual, Mr. Booth."

"And you are a shit-eating pig."

Stanton gave no indication that he was affected by the insult. Instead, he shoved the derringer into a coat pocket and studied me silently. "I have to be honest; I was more than slightly perturbed when the lieutenant informed me that the body he retrieved from Garrett's farm wasn't yours. Even more so when he told me you were still alive. But then he explained as to how you had spared his life on the T.B. Road, and for that, Mr. Booth, I am admittedly grateful. The lieutenant is a valuable man, and not easily replaced."

"Truly?" Despite my fear, and Luther's hovering presence, I managed a snorting laugh. "Not even when you have the entire sewer at your disposal?"

The Secretary was not amused. "Do not condemn that which you do not understand. You should be thankful to the Almighty that you are still alive. I have never had you out of my grasp, sir. Not since this entire affair began. I could have killed you at any time of my choosing."

"And why is that, Mr. Stanton?" My anger was rapidly replacing my trepidation. "Why should I have been hunted like a dog in the first place? You and I had an agreement, did we not? As long as I carried out your nefarious scheme, my life would be spared. Well, sir, I did as you asked. I killed your Mr. Lincoln. Why was I betrayed?"

His blank expression never wavered. "If you recall, sir, our agreement had two parts; I was to spare you only if you remained silent." He opened the satchel once again and pulled out a pair of flat objects. One was my diary. The other was the envelope I had given to John Matthews.

And I was not the least surprised to see either.

Stanton held up both. "And as you can see, Mr. Booth, you did not keep your end of the bargain." He reached inside the envelope and tugged out my letter, slowly folding it open in his small hands. "Your friend Mr. Matthews was understandably upset, once he witnessed your leap from that theater box. He had the good sense to turn this over to my detectives. Fortunately for him, he did not open it. But I did." He glanced over the letter with pursed, speculative lips. "Eloquent, of course, although considering your talent I would have expected no less."

"And you brought me here to offer your praise?" I forced a sardonic sneer. "How touching."

"Praise?" Stanton glanced up at me over the letter. "Hardly the word I would have chosen. What was it your own Mr. Shakespeare said? I come not to praise Caesar, but to bury him? No, sir, my time is far too valuable to be wasted on cheap theatrics." He shook the documents in my direction. "Why, Mr. Booth?"

"Because I don't like being lied to! Or threatened!"

"Ah," Stanton nodded understandingly. "Then that is where you made your greatest mistake. There is a distinct difference between a threat and a promise. I make promises, Mr. Booth. Which I always keep."

I held his grim stare. "You mean you intend to hang Mrs. Surratt?"

He tucked the diary and the letter back into his case. "Her life is of no further consequence to you. None whatsoever. Neither is Mr. Herold's, or any of your other companions'. The President is dead, the public is justifiably outraged, and the perpetrators must be brought to justice. It's as simple as that."

"But she's innocent! She had nothing to do with any of this! My God, sir, you cannot hang an innocent woman!"

Stanton loosed a frustrated sigh. "None of you are innocent, Mr. Booth. Guilt by association is still guilt, at least in the eyes of the law. There is absolutely nothing that can be done for any of them, now."

"Dear God." I had to look away, so terrible was the sudden rush of anguish. I pictured the sweet woman's face in my mind, framed by the evil loop of a hangman's noose. "Forgive me, dear lady," I whispered bitterly. "Please, forgive me."

"What was that, Mr. Booth?"

I shook my head, trying desperately to summon what little dignity I still possessed. "You told me Lincoln was planning to destroy the South," I finally managed to croak. "Was that a lie, Mr. Stanton?"

"A regrettable falsehood," he nodded slowly, "but one that was necessary to insure your participation. Mr. Lincoln was a complex man, Mr. Booth. He was courageous, and dedicated, and, even I must admit, capable of absolute brilliance. It pains me to say it, as much as I truly detested the man, but I doubt sincerely that the Union would have won this war under another man's leadership. But once it was over, he had no true understanding of how the freedom we had just vouchsafed had to be preserved."

The Secretary began another of his short, anxious paces in the wavering light. "You see, Mr. Booth, I, too, am a patriot, just as you claim to be. I love this country greater than my own life. To stand idly by and watch while the traitors who had attempted to tear it asunder were allowed to go unpunished; well, I'm afraid that was far too much for me, and many others here in Washington, to blithely accept. We tried to explain to Mr. Lincoln that his policy of forgiveness simply wouldn't work. He would only be enticing other like-minded anarchists to further rebellion. But he was obsessed with his wretched notion of charity."

Stanton's thin lips curled in livid contempt. "Charity!" He repeated the word, fairly hissing through clenched teeth. "I must have heard him utter that God-damned word nearly a thousand times a day! But I'm afraid I am not a charitable man, sir, not when it comes to treason. How in God's Name did he expect us to continue as a nation? Even an unruly child responds promptly, and properly, to harsh chastisement!" He shook his gray head slowly, glancing up at me. "So in order to save the Union a second time, Mr. Booth, it became unfortunately necessary to remove the president."

"But why me?" Despite Luther Baker's ominous proximity, it was becoming all I could do to keep from summoning one final surge of strength and pouncing on the bastard. "Why me, Mr. Stanton? Why was I the one chosen to carry out your filthy plan? Answer me, God damn you! Why did it have to be me?"

Stanton shrugged, almost blithely. "Because you were perfect, Mr. Booth. Absolutely perfect. Arrogant, vainglorious, fanatical. My God, sir, I could not have molded you to greater perfection had you been made of clay. When Colonel Baker first informed me of your kidnap plot, I wanted to hang you and your vile band without so much as a trial. But then, after I had read his reports, I knew that I had discovered the ideal assassin." He shook an admonishing finger at me. "I told you, sir; there is a Divine hand at work in all of this. We would be fools to ignore it."

Arrogant. Vainglorious. Fanatical. The words knifed into my soul like a flaming sword, more painful than the throb in my leg. And they were all the more excruciating because of their damnable truth.

I leaned on the crutch and shook my head, praying for an end to this unholy nightmare. "And when he thinks, good easy man, full surely his greatness is a-ripening, nips his root, then falls as I do. Shakespeare," I sighed, glancing up at Stanton. "Henry the Eighth, act three, scene two. You would enjoy it, Mr. Stanton. I believe it was written with you in mind."

"Sweet Christ!" The Secretary rolled his dark eyes. "Always the actor, aren't you? So wretchedly melodramatic! Well, then, allow me to present a tableau of my own." He waved a hand towards the shallow grave. "Tell me, sir; who do you think lies in that grave?"

I swept my eyes across the stiffening corpse, remembering the pleasant, innocent face of the hapless Maryland sergeant. "Rhodie," I sighed, glaring back at Stanton. "His name was Rhodie."

"On the contrary," Stanton said, obviously relishing his little performance. "His name is John Wilkes Booth."

I could only gape at him. "What?"

Stanton nodded slowly. "That's right, Mr. Booth. I'm not going to kill you. After all, you've done your country a great service. They may not realize it now, perhaps not even for some years to come. But they will, sir, they will. And when they do, they'll have you to thank."

"Bastard!" I hissed the word between my teeth, finally losing all control, I stumbled forward, as swiftly as the crutch would permit, fully intending to choke the life out of him. "You miserable bastard!"

My assault was quickly halted, and painfully, as Luther Baker's outstretched hand suddenly closed around my throat. The giant would have snapped my neck like a twig had not Stanton waved him off.

"Enough, lieutenant," the Secretary said calmly. "Let him go. If Mr. Booth wishes to play the fool and throw his life away, then you'll have him soon enough."

Luther reluctantly shoved me backwards, a disappointed glare in his eyes.

I managed to keep my balance, but it was several moments before I could draw breath enough to speak. I rubbed at my throat, shaking my head at Stanton. "I don't understand. Why the hell would you let me live? What makes you think I would ever stay silent? That I won't go to the newspapers, or just write another goddamned letter?"

"Because you won't," he replied simply. "You know as well as I do that the fate which will shortly befall your companions can easily be extended to others, especially those closest to you. Your own brothers, for example?" He held up a single stubby finger. "But all of that aside, Mr. Booth, I still have one unequivocal assurance of your complete silence. You are now a hero to your precious South. A glorious martyr to a fallen cause. Imagine that stature, should they ever discover the truth as to why you really killed

Abraham Lincoln? Considering your monstrous vanity, sir, I seriously doubt you would ever compromise such acclaim." He pointed to the grave once again, and his dark eyes held me with a flat, contemptuous stare that was a thing of pure evil. "The choice is yours, Mr. Booth. Though I'm reasonably certain as to which one you'll make."

The silence in that hideous chamber grew coldly malignant. I stared back at him, trying desperately to force some sort of utterance from my slack and paralyzed jaw. Had he pierced my body with white-hot irons, then flayed the very flesh from my bones, the agony could hardly have been greater. For I knew, beyond all possible doubt, that the son of a bitch was right.

Stanton reached into his pocket, tugging Prudy's little pistol once more into view. He held it in his open palm and frowned at it thoughtfully. "This weapon truly belongs in a museum, though I haven't the slightest idea as to how I would explain its presence. I suppose we'll just have to make do with the other." He threw the gun to me, with a sudden flick of his small fingers. "You keep it, Mr. Booth, as a souvenir. Along with that money you tried to hoodwink from me."

He chuckled at my stupefied gape.

"Nothing escapes me, sir. When my agents in Canada informed me of the transfer, I admit I was slightly piqued. I could easily seize your accounts, believe me. But I enjoy matching wits with an occasional adversary, though I must admit your talents are, shall we say, woefully lacking. As far as I'm concerned, you earned that money." He fastened the buckles on his satchel and glanced at Luther Baker. "There's a small steamer berthed across the river at Alexandria, lieutenant. It leaves on the morning tide for New Orleans. Please see Mr. Booth safely aboard. What happens to him after that is his own affair."

Stanton turned away from both of us, slowly trudging

towards the steps. "You have your country's thanks, Mr. Booth, as well as your money. Enjoy them both, courtesy of Edwin Stanton . . . ."

Chapter Nineteen

I will answer well this death I gave him,
So again good night; this bad begins
And worse remains behind.
               ---Hamlet---

Granbury, Texas - September 1876

"So you see, Finis, I am dead."

St. Helen turned his head slightly, staring bleakly at me. "Dead to the all that matters, at least. All that remains is to shuffle off this mortal coil, which I pray to God is damnably soon."

"Jesus God." I had to sit back, reeling in utter astonishment. I was convinced, of course, that his entire tale had been fabricated, merely the ravings of a fevered brain. And yet, there was something about it that rang so inexorably true. I stared at his pale face, so drawn and sullen in the lamplight, and tried to sort it all out.

"Truly, John, you have to admit this is hard to fathom."

He eyed me desperately. "Yet it's true, Finis! Before God, you must believe me!" He reached out and grabbed at my arm. "You must!"

"Please, John, calm yourself," I nodded as I gently patted the trembling hand. "I didn't say that I didn't believe you. But tell me, how did you end up here, in Texas?"

"I didn't come here right away. It was a while, actually. A long while. After I arrived in New Orleans, I went to see a doctor. My leg had indeed healed quite wretchedly, just as I feared, but I found a good man who was competent enough to repair the damage. I could afford it," he said grimly. "After all, I had six hundred thousand dollars."

"The money was actually waiting for you?"

"Oh, yes, every penny. Stanton had kept his promise. Just as he kept another." His face hardened in bitter, anguished fury. "He hanged them, Finis. The bastard went and hanged them. George, Lewis, and poor, gentle Davey. And Widow Surratt. Yet the son of a bitch wasn't content to let it stop with that. He sent Dr. Mudd to prison, just for setting my leg. And Ned Spangler, too. Poor Neddy went up for helping me to hold my horse that night, but his real crime was simply that he knew me. Even Sam Arnold and Michael O'Laughlin ended up in a Yankee dungeon, and they hadn't even been part of the murder plot. Only John Surratt escaped, though the little coward let his mother hang in his stead."

"But what about Davey," I demanded anxiously. "He knew you weren't dead. Why didn't he talk?"

"A lot of people knew I wasn't dead," St. Helen said tersely. "The few people, and they were precious few, Finis, who actually saw that body knew that it wasn't me. Yet who was willing to oppose Edwin Stanton? Davey didn't talk for fear the butcher would have hanged his mother and sisters. And who's to say he wouldn't have? The bastard swung up the dear widow!"

I eyed him evenly, candidly. "Is that why you did it, John? Did you kill Lincoln just to try and save Mrs. Surratt?"

St. Helen turned to glare at me, and in his eyes was the most pained expression I had ever seen in my entire life. "Is that what you think, Finis? Is it? For if it is, then let me assure you, you could not be more wrong. I killed Lincoln to save my own worthless neck. Not for Mrs. Surratt, not for the South, and not for Stanton's contemptible money! I did it solely for the miserable life of John Wilkes Booth." He tried to force a cynical chuckle, but the sound that emerged was more akin to a sob. "Such a magnificently noble cause, don't you think?"

He fell back against his pillow, and the little room fell

deathly silent. I watched as a pastiche of emotions suddenly flickered across St. Helen's drawn face, as though he were recalling a myriad of images. It was several long moments before he spoke again.

"Stanton knew exactly what he was doing by letting me live," he said with a sigh. "He put me in hell. He knew damned well I would have to be witness to all of it."

I shook my head, confused. "All of what, John?"

"Reconstruction. And I saw everything, Finis. Every last horror. Once my leg had healed, I traveled across the South; first to Vicksburg, then further east, to Atlanta. Everywhere I went, I saw those good people robbed of every shred of dignity, every ounce of self-respect. And after a while, I simply couldn't stand to see any more. So I came here to Texas, where the war had been far less taxing."

He could no longer restrain bitter tears. "You know, Finis, it's damnably odd, but they say I shouted, '*sic semper tyrannis*,' when I leaped from that box. I've often wondered as to how that rumor actually began. I never said anything, not a single wretched word; yet to the South, it was almost a battle cry. Stanton had actually been right. As far as they were concerned, John Wilkes Booth had given his very life to try and avenge their affliction. Jesus Christ." His entire body began to heave with desperate, uncontrollable sobs. "John Wilkes Booth was their Judas."

"John, please." I reached out to try and take his hand, but he pulled it away, swiftly fighting to regain his composure.

"I'll be all right, Finis. Sometimes it just seems far too much to bear, that's all. Thank God it'll all be over soon." He wiped at his face with a corner of the heavy quilt. "Dear God, how many times I've wished that Prudy had had the nerve to put that bullet through my brain! The same bullet I used to kill Abe Lincoln. Who knows how different things might have been? Who knows what might have happened, had I not been the instrument of darkness."

He dropped his head back again with a rasping sigh. "Too much," I heard him whisper. "Far too much." He offered me a weary smile. "I'm afraid I'm greatly fatigued now, dear Finis. Perhaps you can come again tomorrow? If I'm still alive, of course."

"Don't worry, John," I tried to reassure him, remembering the night's earlier crisis. "All you need is a little rest. You'll be as good as new in no time." I stood up to go.

St. Helen's eyes flew open. "Finis, you've got to promise me you won't repeat a word of what I told you."

I nodded swiftly. "I gave you my word, John. I won't break it."

"And you'll tell my brother Edwin of my death?"

"I shall inform him personally, even if I have to travel to New York."

He seemed satisfied at that. "Then I shall try to sleep. If I don't see you again, Finis, I want you to know how grateful I am for all your help. And your friendship."

I had to choke back the sudden lump in my throat. "You are an easy man to befriend, John."

"No," he said sadly, blinking at another flow of tears. "I am a wretched fool. But I'll ask of you the same thing I asked of Prudy, Finis; please don't think of me with hatred. I have lost all that was ever precious to me. I cannot bear to lose anymore."

He closed his eyes and was soon asleep.

I left Mrs. Grady's with a spinning head. I was still certain that St. Helen's story was contrived, yet I had to confess I was more than slightly intrigued. What little I knew of Lincoln's death was the same as anyone else, and the facts, at least those the world had been given, seemed plausible enough. But to think that the government itself could be responsible for a president's death? I shook my head with a sardonic chuckle.

The idea was completely ludicrous. Even in Texas.

I meant to return to Mrs. Grady's the next morning, but an urgent telegram from the Federal court in Tyler summoned me to a murder trial in Smith County. I had to leave without seeing St. Helen, and it was nearly two weeks before I could return to Granbury. I sent Mrs. Grady a telegram, inquiring of St. Helen's health, but received nothing in reply. Perhaps her felonious offspring had purloined the cable. But I made it a point, once the stagecoach had rolled to a dusty halt in the Granbury square, to hurry along Pearl Street to the Grady house.

The good lady was washing a spatter of red mud from the front wall as I trotted up the porch steps. Apparently her sons had decided the regular color was unattractive, and had taken steps to remedy the matter. She threw me a flustered smile from beneath a dusty kerchief.

"Why, hello, Mr. Bates. I haven't seen you in several days."

"Mrs. Grady. Always busy, I see."

She nodded, and rather bleakly. "Always." She peered at me with a sudden, anxious frown. "Have you heard from Mr. St. Helen, by any chance?"

I stopped dead in my tracks. "Have I heard? What do you mean, Mrs. Grady? Why should I have heard from Mr. St. Helen?"

She shook her rag-encircled head. "I had hoped that after he left he might have tried to contact you, given you're such good friends."

"After he left?"

"Yes. He packed up and left about a week ago, Mr. Bates. One morning he came down to breakfast and said that he was feeling a great deal better, and that afternoon he was gone." She snapped soapy fingers. "Just like that. No one here in town has seen or heard from him, not even Mr. Gordon."

I could not believe it. "Did he where he was going, or why?"

"Not a word," she sighed. "No one even saw him leave. He left his rent money on the dining table, and a significant amount extra. I was greatly overwhelmed, but then he always was a generous man. Mr. Gordon and I were hoping you might have heard something, Mr. Bates, but I take it you haven't?"

"No," I rasped. "Nothing. Tell me, Mrs. Grady, did Mr. St. Helen say anything to you before he left? While he was still sick, I mean?"

She thought for a moment. "Not that I can recall. He did leave a small pouch behind, which I thought was rather strange."

"Why is that?"

"It was sitting in the middle of his bed," she explained. "All by itself. He had taken everything else, which is why I couldn't understand him leaving the packet."

"Do you still have it?" I asked quickly. "I mean, might it be possible for me to see it?"

"Of course. Wait a moment and I'll fetch it out."

She tossed a sopping rag into a bucket of dirty water and quickly went inside. I waited on the porch in a virtual state of stunned bewilderment.

"Here we are," Mrs. Grady chirped as she returned. "I haven't opened it, since he had left me all that money. I didn't really feel it was my business."

I took the little pouch, the same one that had held the mysterious photographs, and opened the drawstrings with eager but trembling hands. Inside, there was a small object wrapped in a faded piece of newspaper.

Mrs. Grady watched curiously as I unwrapped the paper. "My goodness!" she exclaimed. "Look at the headline, Mr. Bates! That paper is from the war!"

I stared at the boldfaced type, and its grim proclamation of Lincoln's death, and my disbelieving eyes flicked to the small, metallic object resting in my left palm.

It was a derringer; a Brown, according to the faded letters etched into the rusted metal, with a short barrel that swiveled open when I pressed a tiny lever.

Mrs. Grady frowned over the pistol. "Well, now, would you look at that! Why in the world do you think Mr. St. Helen would leave a gun behind, Mr. Bates? Mr. Bates?"

But I could not answer her. Nor could I, in fact, find any voice at all. I was far too enraptured in the single brass cartridge I had pulled from the breech of the pistol. A cartridge that was tarnished, and corroded.

And empty.

– THE END –

Author's Notes

There really was a John St. Helen, and his story, of Booth's supposed escape, is very much as the novel has portrayed. But St. Helen's claim that he, as John Wilkes Booth, was a part of a government plot to kill Abraham Lincoln is by no means unique to the Texas barkeep.

That Booth killed Lincoln is irrefutable. That there was a conspiracy in the president's death, however limited, is also without dispute. Four persons; Lewis Paine, George Atzerodt, David Herold, and Mary Surratt, went to the gallows on July 7th, 1865, for their supposed complicity in the President's murder. Several others, including Dr. Samuel Mudd and Edmund Spangler, spent an irretrievable portion of their lives in Ft. Jefferson prison, in the Dry Tortugas, America's equivalent to Devil's Island. According to documented history, each one of these individuals played a small but important role in the tragedy enacted at Ford's.

Yet from the very night of the assassination, a number of mysterious occurrences took place that have never been fully explained. One of the most significant was the confusion surrounding Lincoln's bodyguard. Or, more accurately, the lack thereof.

Edwin Stanton had warned Gen. Ulysses Grant, Lincoln's first choice for a theater companion, to leave Washington the day of the assassination, citing a threat of imminent danger to Grant's life. Stanton's same caution was issued, to a lesser degree, to the president himself, but when Lincoln reluctantly agreed to a bodyguard, specifically requesting Major Thomas Eckert (Stanton's chief of the War Department telegraph office), his request was denied. Eckert, Stanton explained, had to work late that night, and was therefore unavailable. But when the government offices shut down, at five p.m. that evening, both Eckert and Stanton went home. No one worked late at the War Department.

The man eventually assigned to protect the President and Mrs.

Lincoln was a drunken, disreputable D.C. police officer named John Parker, a man who had already been cited some fourteen times for dereliction of duty. The Lincolns had no sooner taken their seats at the theater when Parker promptly disappeared, ending up drunk in a nearby tavern. He was never sanctioned, disciplined, or even reprimanded for deserting his post.

A second, even more baffling question concerns Stanton's possible knowledge of Booth's kidnap plot. Louis Wiechmann, the young divinity student who roomed at Mrs. Surratt's knew of the plot from his friendship with John Surratt. Wiechmann told another friend, a pro-Union War Department clerk named Gleason, possibly as early as January of 1865. That Gleason did not inform his superiors seems almost unthinkable. Adding credence to this theory is the fact that less than two hours after Lincoln had been shot, and while several hundred witnesses still argued as to exactly who it was that had leaped from the Presidential box, Secretary Stanton had issued arrest warrants for each and every one of Booth's co-conspirators. It would not have been possible, given the slipshod police techniques of the time, for him to have identified these individuals without some prior knowledge.

But the third, and perhaps the most damning evidence against Stanton is the infamous Booth diary. It was the diary that first cast suspicion on the Secretary of War, during the impeachment trial of Andrew Johnson.

Johnson, an alcoholic weakling with close ties to his native Tennessee, had been charged by the pro-Union government with being too lenient on the South during the hellish years of Reconstruction. Ironically, Johnson himself was thought by many to have been involved with Lincoln's death, owing to the mysterious note Booth left for him at the Kirkwood Hotel (an event which has still yet to be sufficiently explained). A congressional committee subpoenaed the diary, which was in Stanton's possession, but the Secretary vehemently refused to relinquish the book. When he finally yielded—only after being threatened with an obstruction of justice charge—the panel discovered that eighteen pages of Booth's daybook had been torn out. Stanton insisted that the pages had always been missing, a claim which several War Department officials openly disputed. Years later, after his death, the Secretary's personal effects were being catalogued by family members, and several pages of the diary were discovered. They reportedly contained a list of prominent names, of both pro-Southern and pro-Northern individuals, whom Booth claimed were involved with Lincoln's assassination. Stanton's name was conspicuously absent.

It was no secret, even at that time, that Edwin Stanton hated Abraham Lincoln. Lincoln's oldest son, Robert, made the claim in later life that his father's death had not been the act of a single fanatic, and that Stanton had known far more than he was willing to admit. Stanton, Speaker of the House Thaddeus Stevens, and a number of Lincoln's cabinet had openly opposed many of the President's policies, most notably the plan for a peaceful Reconstruction. The theory that Lincoln had been murdered because of this unpopular policy was the subject of persistent Washington rumors for years following the assassination.

As Secretary of War, Stanton's power was immense, and ironically made so by Lincoln's wartime suspension of habeas corpus. He had command over a small army of fiercely loyal intelligence operatives, or "detectives," and it would not have been impossible for him to have arranged the death of any individual, including the President. It has been estimated that, during the course of the Civil War, Stanton was responsible for the arrest and imprisonment of more than two hundred thousand people; scores of whom did, in fact, simply disappear.

There is other compelling evidence to suggest a broader conspiracy. That night in Ford's, Booth did give fellow actor John Matthews a sealed packet, with the explicit instructions to deliver it to the *National Intelligencer* the next morning. Matthews is purported to have read the enclosed document the night Lincoln died, and supposedly burned the entire contents in horror. This may or may not have been true, since he only ever revealed vague reports of the letter, preferring to keep a wary silence. But it is absolutely certain the letter disappeared.

And—just as St. Helen explained to Finis Bates—the body pulled from Garrett's tobacco barn was the subject of fierce controversy. The face was badly disfigured, though whether from a bullet or fire was never ascertained. The military held a brief, cursory "autopsy," aboard an ironclad anchored in the Potomac, and only a handful of select witnesses were permitted to see the corpse. Several, including Booth's own doctor, initially refused to identify the body as that of the famous actor, and did so only at the government's heated insistence. But no one from Booth's family, not even his own brothers, ever laid eyes on the body until long after it had rotted away to a skeleton. Cousins LaFayette and Luther Baker, who headed the manhunt for Booth—and later split a sizable share of the reward money—secretly buried the corpse in the basement of Washington's Old Arsenal Penitentiary, where it remained until after Stanton's death in 1869.

David Herold did indeed make the insistent claim that the man who was killed in Garrett's barn was not Booth, but was ordered by several individuals, including his own lawyer, to keep his mouth shut. On the scaffold, Lewis Paine made the cryptic statement that "they ain't caught the half of us, yet." Paine also insisted that Mrs. Surratt was completely innocent. The evidence also seemed to indicate that conclusion, yet she was still executed, despite desperate pleas for clemency by dozens of noted Washington dignitaries. The conspirators' trial had been held before a military tribunal—under Stanton's ironclad authority—but the officers who voted unanimously to convict the widow later insisted, to a man, that they never expected her ro hang. Anna Surratt, the widow's daughter, was physically barred from entering the White House to plead with President Johnson by two pro-Union senators, Preston King of New York, and James Lane of Kansas. Both men had extremely close ties to Edwin Stanton, and both would inexplicably commit suicide less than a year later. Theirs would not be the only mysterious deaths to arise from the tragedy. Less than two years after the assassination, Col. LaFayette Baker died of what many believe was poisoning, shortly after reporting to close friends that he had evidence that would prove government involvement in the president's death. One theory holds that he was trying to blackmail Edwin Stanton.

John Surratt, the widow's son, was the only member of Booth's band to escape Stanton's clutches. He ran first to Canada, then later to England, and finally ended up in Rome, where he became a member of the Papal Guards. He was recognized and arrested by American authorities in 1867, and returned to Washington to stand trial. But by this time, Stanton's authority had weakened, and Surratt went before a civilian jury, who were unable to render a verdict. He spent the rest of his life denying any complicity in the assassination, and offering weak excuses for deserting his unfortunate mother.

As for Dr. Mudd (who was sentenced to life), Ned Spangler, Sam Arnold, and Michael O'Laughlin; they were originally slated to spend their incarceration in the Federal penitentiary near Albany, New York. But at the last minute, they were rerouted to the tropical hell of Ft. Jefferson. The man responsible for that order was Edwin Stanton. In 1867, O'Laughlin died during a yellow fever epidemic that swept the island prison. Dr. Mudd, who risked his own life to treat inmates and guards alike, was subsequently pardoned by Andrew Johnson. Spangler and Arnold were released shortly thereafter, and by 1869, the last of Lincoln's accused assassins were free. And the government's case was officially closed.

One final, yet still deeply puzzling detail concerns the endless funds to which Booth supposedly had access, especially when coupled with the incredible wealth of which John St. Helen openly boasted. By early 1865, Booth's acting career was on the wane, owing to his failing voice, yet his wallet was never empty. He lavished a small fortune on the kidnap plot, much of which came from Canada, through the assistance of Jacob Thompson. Thompson, a

Mississippian who had once served as Secretary of the Interior under President James Buchanan, severed his Union ties early in the war and went to Canada, where he became a key member of the notorious "Canadian Cabinet." Run by the Richmond government, the group was responsible for numerous acts of sabotage in Northern cities, and channeled funds to the Confederacy from England and France. Shortly before Lincoln's murder, the Canadian accounts—to which Booth had immediate access—inexplicably swelled to more than $600,000. Yet by the morning of the assassination, virtually every penny had disappeared. The war Department issued a warrant for Thompson's arrest, but, like Surratt, Thompson escaped to England, where he spent the remainder of his life. Any answers he might have provided concerning the missing money went with him.

Did John Wilkes Booth survive that burning barn to become a Texas bartender? The answer is . . . maybe. John St. Helen made a significant claim, which Finis Bates spent the better part of his life—and his personal funds—attempting to prove. After St. Helen disappeared from Granbury, Bates refused to rest until he had located his old friend, as well as proof that St. Helen had not been lying. Bates found two elderly Union veterans, both of whom had been on duty at the Navy Yard Bridge the night of the assassination. Both men told the lawyer that a man matching Booth's description had indeed ridden across the bridge unimpeded, after giving the officer in charge a mysterious password; "T.B. Road." Later, in 1903, Bates learned of a man named David George who had committed suicide in Enid, Oklahoma, but only after claiming to be none other than John Wilkes Booth. Bates went to Enid and claimed the body, which he later had mummified, and was convinced that George and St. Helen were one and the same. He had several doctors examine the corpse, and they found substantial physical evidence that seemed to support George/St. Helen's claim. The body had a poorly healed broken left leg, facial features that matched photographs of Booth, and, more importantly, bore a surgical scar on the back of the neck which Booth's own doctor could not find on the Garrett corpse. After Bates' death, the mummy fell into the possession of a carnival sideshow, and was exhibited at southern state fairs and circuses until sometime in the nineteen-forties. It disappeared for several years after that, but recently turned up in the hands of a Tennessee doctor.

The St. Helen story lingered in limbo, just another tall Texas tale, and probably would have stayed there, until the fall of 1994, when lawyers for Booth's descendants filed a petition in Baltimore federal court to have the assassin's body exhumed from Baltimore's Greenmount Cemetery for comprehensive DNA testing. The George/St. Helen claims figured prominently in their affidavits, along with other evidence which the family insists has left an unending anxiety over just who it is that actually lies buried within the Booth vault. But the mystery seems slated to continue, following a federal judge's ruling in May of 1995, that the proffered evidence was far too vague to justify the time and expense of such an examination.

Was John St. Helen really John Wilkes Booth? And was Booth really the "instrument of darkness"? The answer may never be known. Unlike the Kennedy assassination, all of the key performers and witnesses to Lincoln's death are long gone. All that remains are theories. But then, theories often make for terrific novels . . .

— Rusty Harding

Made in the USA
Lexington, KY
25 November 2015